Between Sisters

Book One

Queendom Dreams Publishing
PO Box 93832,
Las Vegas, NV 89193

Printed in the United States of America

First Edition

ISBN-13: 978-0-9827-2231-2
ISBN-10: 0-9827-2231-X

Cover Design: Candace Cottrell
Editing & Typesetting: Carla Dean of U Can Mark My Word

For information regarding special ordering for bulk purchases, contact: Queendom Dreams Publishing, PO Box 93832, Las Vegas, NV 89193

Website: www.queendomdreams.com

Acknowledgements

First and foremost, I give all honor and thanks unto Jehovah God. It almost seems like an oxymoron to mention God in such a profane book, but without His grace, no talent I have been blessed with would come to fruition. I thank Him for giving me the ability to give people what it is they crave through my writings...past, present and future.

Thank you to the women who had a strong hand in molding me into the woman I am today. By name, they are the late: Linnette Tompkins-Stallings, Anna Franke, Catherine Carlton, Lona Cole, Mabel 'Omar' Butler, and Jessie Mae Butler. Still amongst the living are: my aunts Marsha Butler and Lois Clark. Each has so richly been a blessing in my life.

Along my path, I have been privileged to meet some absolutely wonderful people who played a very instrumental role in my life. Listed by state: (NY/NJ) Tanya Tompkins-Williams, Patricia Brown, Felton Caviness, Kevin 'Sugar Daddy' Woodley, Lorene Young, (VA) Marjorie "Neicy" Tate, (MD) Jamie Peace, Veronica Nash, Heidi Devane, Steffany Powell, and Tanya McCain. Thank you all for having my back and showing me what True Friendship is really about.

I have to also thank those who have randomly been chosen over the years for MY PANEL. (Getting selected to be on my panel is about the equivalent of getting jury duty selection). I appreciate your cooperation.

I must give a shoutout to our former President that helped the country into a horrible recession, which finally left me with idle time on my hands (from being unemployed) long enough to complete three book to date. Big thanks to ya! Talk about making lemonade from lemons. It was a long fall from grace, but that's okay. Out of it comes strength, humility, and resilience. A brilliant diamond must go through the fire for better clarity.

Although they have no idea who I am or remember who I am, I have to show my love for Keith Sweat, R. Kelly, Johnny Gill, Joe, the late Teddy Pendergrass & Barry White, The Whispers, Euge Groove, Peter White, Bob Baldwin, Boney James, and Spur of the Moment. As I would write and tune out the rest of the world, I kept my iPod in my ears with you all at some point or another, inspiring or influencing my thought process. Thanks for helping to transcend my mind onto an erotic journey.

Gotta give a shoutout to Pookie and Ray-Ray and Junebug and Ruff-Ruff... (Just kidding!) Isn't that the common shoutout?

Finally, I can't close without acknowledging where it all began for me: Queensbridge. There began the many nights I'd sit in my window overlooking the Manhattan skyline, along with the Queensboro Bridge (aka 59th Street Bridge), and I'd escape to my fantasy world that I'd often incorporate in my early childhood creative writings. (I used to pretend I was a Queen and the sparkling lights of the bridge were my sparkling diamond necklace). Growing up in projects that contained ninety-six buildings provided me with endless stories to create and write over the years. I've had twenty-five years of great memories there and many years to be groomed into that Queen. So, in a nutshell, Queensbridge is who I am, and now I shall go on as The Queen…

Between Sisters

Book One

The Queen

Queendom Dreams Publishing
www.queendomdreams.com

Prologue

1

"I'm getting sick of going to the jazz club each week for girls' night out. The same damn club week after week. D.C. has too many spots to go to. Why can't we do something different sometimes?"

"Kelly, you know how your sister is. She acts like none of us have enough sense to decide on something else."

"You have always been Elaine's favorite. Why don't you tell her we want to do something different this week, Shawnee?"

"PULEASE! How do you figure that? Elaine Wiggins is all about herself. *She* is her only favorite. Besides, it's not just Elaine. I guess you forgot about your other sisters. We'd still have to check with Harmony and Charise, and be glad Sandy is not around. Otherwise, you'd have to check with her, also."

"I already know Charise wants to do something different. We've been talking about it forever. As for Harmony, Momma birthed that girl without a backbone. She'll do whatever."

"That is so not cool, Kelly. How are you going to talk about Harmony like that, when she always comes to your rescue each time you get in some mess? When you bought that new Land Rover straight off the showroom floor that had your ass stuck on the side of the road a couple of months ago—in the middle of the night no less—while coming back from Detroit, who came for your silly behind because you forgot to renew your AAA?" Shawnee chuckled. "Furthermore, Harmony is not one to sleep on. She'll dropkick all of your asses in a heartbeat."

Kelly laughed. "Okay, you're right. To be honest, I think none of us have a backbone when it comes to Elaine."

"Tell me this since you're closer in age to Elaine than I am, and I pretty much was gone while you all were coming up. How in the hell did she become so damn mean and spoiled? Is that a Taurus thing? Hell, I don't remember her ever getting her way with Momma."

"It must be her Taurus trait 'cause she never got her way with Momma. Daddy was the one always buying her stuff, and Momma was the one she was always fighting with. I guess she figured she could go a few rounds with Momma, so now she thinks she can walk all over everyone else."

"Oh hell no! Wilhelmina Josie Mae Wyatt-Wiggins never let Elaine walk all over her." That is the way Shawnee would often refer to their mother, with her strong personality and whom they feared greatly while growing up. "Shoot, while Momma was on her deathbed just two years ago, I still was afraid of her kicking my ass. That woman was no joke," Shawnee laughed.

Kelly slightly laughed before shifting into a whiney voice. "Yeah, but whatever the case, we need to do something about this girls' night out thing. We've been going to this same spot for over a year now. Shawnee, you're the oldest. You should be the one stepping up and changing the order."

"Kelly, I have a good husband, a nice home that I don't mind spending my free time in, and a great job. I wouldn't even be out in the streets if it weren't for us trying to keep our pact since Momma's death of always having girls' night out once a week. Sandy broke our pact already. She packed up and moved clear across the country with her family when she got married."

"That's because Sandy's dog of a husband, Lewis, was always hitting on every damn body, and she couldn't stand us always getting on her case about giving him the boot. She's content living in her fantasy world and thinks moving to Denver is going to help his cheating ways."

Shawnee laughed heartedly. "Yeah, and she moves him to the same town where black men are scarce and in high demand." She paused for a moment and then shared, "Hmm, now that I think about it, Sandy met Lewis at that same jazz club. I would hate for any of my other sisters to end up with a loser from that club."

"And don't forget about Elaine now hooked up with that broke down sax player," Kelly threw in.

"Well, at least he doesn't try hitting on everyone like Lewis does, and that 'broke down sax player' loves him some Elaine."

"Shawnee, we shouldn't be forced to go to the jazz club just because Elaine is screwing the sax player. When do the rest of us get to just let loose and have a good time? I feel like the oldest twenty-six year-old, sitting week after week with a bunch of stuffy old-ass men, while they swirl around their brandy and don't have a damn thing in common to talk about. To be honest, I don't even like jazz. I tolerate it," Kelly pouted through the phone.

Shawnee laughed. "Oh, but you love those 'old men', as you call them, when they send us drinks for the table. See if any young guy will do that."

"Well…" Kelly couldn't help but to laugh, also. "Okay, so they're good for something. I'm just saying… Let's do different things sometimes."

"Alright! Alright! I'm sold. Get with Charise and Harmony to decide where we will go this week. I think we will be switching things up from now on."

"Yay!" Kelly squealed with excitement, clapping her hands like a small child. "Will you be letting Elaine know she won't be calling the shots anymore?"

"I got this, Kelly. Now, I have to get back to work. I've had about ten faces at my door trying to talk with me about something. Besides, my soup is getting cold for the third time."

"Soup? In June, Shawnee?"

"Girl, what you talking about? Crab soup is damn good in June."

"Ooh, crab soup. I want some," Kelly playfully begged.

"Yeah, it tastes much better when you don't have to microwave it three, four, and five times because you keep getting interrupted every time you try to eat your lunch," Shawnee laughed.

"That's what comes with being a senior partner in an advertising company."

"This is true, and I wouldn't trade one bit of it for anything. But, those interruptions also come from having too many aggravating sisters working my last nerve with something or other every five minutes."

"Whatever! Not me. Must be all those other sisters," Kelly laughed.

"Uhm-hmm, if you say so," Shawnee laughed with her.

"Well, alright, sis, get back to work. I have contracts to get cracking on anyhow. I'll call you tonight and let you know what we came up with."

"Sounds good. Love you, lil' sis."

"Love you, too," Kelly said, then pressed the off button on her phone and logged into her email account.

Gotta love being my own boss. No one up my ass telling me I can't check my emails anymore. Life is lovely! Kelly thought to herself as she smiled and looked around at the office she created out of the den of her home that she purchased a year after graduating from Howard University three years ago. The home made her mother reiterate her pride in Kelly for doing so well and staying focused to achieve her goals of having her own business and home by the age of twenty-five.

"Junk…delete…delete…delete. Hmm, this looks interesting," she said out loud to herself while clicking on an email titled: 'The Groove Crew Shake Their Moneymaker This Wednesday.'

The email that opened to graphics portraying six exotic dancers read:

Ladies, Come Kick off the Summer With
DC's Hottest Guys, 'The Groove Crew'
Featuring the internationally known:
Mandingo
As They Shake Their Moneymakers

It's All Going Down/Coming Off This Wednesday
At the All-new - Megaplex

Doors Open at 6 p.m., Showtime 7:30 p.m.
2-for-1 Apple Martinis from 6-7 p.m.
Music Provided by DJ Hot-n-Nuff
Gentlemen Welcome for the After Party
9:30 p.m. – 1:00 a.m.
Admission $15 – Ladies, $5 – Men

"WHOOO! WHOOO! Gotta call somebody! Gotta call some damn body!" Hardly able to contain her excitement, Kelly picked up her cell phone to call her youngest sister Charise.

"Hey girl, what's up?" Charise answered when she saw it was Kelly calling.

"Hey, kid! I spoke with Shawnee about doing something different this Wednesday besides the jazz club. She's on board," Kelly said, excited.

"It's about damn time! Shawnee has a husband, so she doesn't care about us poor, single, desperate women."

Kelly squealed. "Well, I have just the thing for us to do this Wednesday. I just received this email, and I must say I was getting kind of excited just reading it. No, let me correct that. I got excited looking at it," said Kelly, fanning herself.

"Ooh! I want to see it. Forward it to me so I can get excited, too. What is it?"

"It's exotic dancers at the Megaplex, the new spot they just opened on New York Avenue. Oh my, they are absolutely gorgeous in this picture. They even have an after party, Charise. You know I'm long overdue to shake my ass."

"Calm down, sis! Now let's get real here. Although I'm all for it, Shawnee's married. She's not going to have it. Elaine is too uptight and probably wouldn't know fun if it came and bit her in the ass. Harmony…well, she'll do whatever, but you know Harmony is quite embarrassing on a dance floor. She has no rhythm whatsoever. I know you haven't forgotten her doing a warp-ass version of the Snake and Cabbage Patch at Shawnee's wedding."

The pair laughed hysterically at the memory of their rhythmless older sister.

"Charise, all we have to do is get Harmony to agree. I'll let Shawnee know what we've come up with, and she'll drag Elaine. It's not like we're asking to see strippers every week. This is only one week."

"Kelly, you don't have to try to convince me. Hell, if it were up to me, I'd say let's find a strip spot every week instead of that bourgeois jazz club we have to go to and act happy. Hell, I'd be happy with a movie or video instead."

Kelly laughed at her sister's sentiments. "I just forwarded the email to you and Harmony. Girl, wait until you see the picture."

"You do know I sit in a stupid cubicle where everyone is all in my conversations, looking over my shoulder all the time, and reading my emails? Everyone keeps looking at me on the phone with you now. Is it safe for me to open, or do I need to check it from home?"

"Charise, you don't have the willpower to wait another four plus hours to see this email?" Kelly joked.

"So what, you're two years older than me and think you know me so well, huh? I might just wait now to prove a point," Charise joked back.

"Correction, I am not two years older. I am twenty-seven months older than you. And no, you can't wait. All of your one-night stands are proof of that," Kelly laughed.

"Ouch! I can't help that I'm a girl who knows what she wants and goes after it," Charise said in her defense. "Why you all up in my business anyhow?"

"Are you kidding?!" Kelly almost choked on the water she was drinking. "How about because you call me after every new dick you get and then want to share the nasty, graphic details. You need to channel some of that one-night-stand energy into your career so you can work your way up from working in a cubicle to having an office with a door."

Charise could feel herself getting annoyed like she always did when she had to defend herself to her big sisters. She always resented being the youngest of her five sisters. To add insult to injury, her nineteen-year-old brother Angelo got on her case as well about her reckless behavior. In her mind, she felt everyone should be happy that she was twenty-four, a University of Maryland graduate, had her own apartment, and didn't have any children compared to Sandy who had three children before turning twenty-two. Each child had a different father and none belonged to her dog-husband who constantly made passes at Charise. Actually, Charise enjoyed the passes Lewis would make and often found herself fantasizing about what he would be like in bed.

Nonetheless, Charise was not in the mood to be lectured by Kelly of all people. Kelly would be the most flirtatious of them all in the jazz club, but when a man approached her, she would whip out her long list of rules that started with the "three-month rule".

On very rare occasions, Kelly and Charise would venture out to Zanzibar, Martini's, or H2O nightclubs together. She couldn't tell anyone that those guys she freaked and rubbed on in the club had to wait three months for her to give up the goodies. Kelly's men typically vanished two weeks later, which according to Charise, was probably when she gave it up.

Charise was ready to end the call. "Kelly, I have to get going now, but count me in for Wednesday," she said, unable to hide her annoyance.

"Okay, heifer. I know you don't want to hear what I have to say, but you know I love you. Anyhow, I'll call Harmony and tell her the plan, and let Shawnee know what we've come up with."

"Your momma's fifth daughter is a heifer," Charise said dryly. "Love you, too, sis."

They both laughed as they ended the call.

Against her better judgment, Shawnee let her younger sister talk her into this "one-time" male stripper party. Not only did she have to get Elaine's hot tempered behind on board, she had to think about what, if anything, she would tell Robert, her husband of four years.

Robert had always been a good husband, until more recently when he started keeping later work hours. Typically, women would say that's the first sign of infidelity. However, with Robert being a corporate attorney, there was no telling. One thing for certain, his late hours and increasing lack of intimacy at home had Shawnee raising her eyebrows.

Shawnee had an equally demanding work schedule, which was why the couple postponed any thoughts of having children, but despite their demanding schedules, they always made time for each other and had regular dates out on the town. Additionally, Shawnee vowed to make time for her sisters' night out once a week. However, this stripper party may have been more than she bargained for.

With no more time to think about it, Shawnee picked up her phone to call Elaine, but not before taking a relaxing hot bubble bath in her large garden tub in front of the large, unobstructed window that offered a spectacular distant view of the bright lights of the Pentagon among other landmarks.

"Hey, big sis, what's going on?" Elaine pleasantly answered upon seeing her sister's number on her caller ID.

"I just got out of my bubble bath."

"Must be nice. Where's Robert?" Elaine asked

"Working, as usual. To tell you the truth, it's getting kind of lonely. When he is home, he's too tired to talk or anything else. And all the little gifts and flowers I used to get seem to not be finding their way to me."

"Wow! I'm sorry to hear that. Hopefully things will get better, but at least we have Wednesday to look forward to."

Shawnee cringed. "Uh…speaking of Wednesday, that's what I'm calling about."

"Don't tell me you can't make it. You know I'm not having that," Elaine said.

"Actually, there's been a change of plans, and everyone else is on board."

Elaine felt an imaginary migraine coming on. "Change, huh? And you say 'everyone' already has made this decision? Was there some family meeting I missed or was deliberately not invited to?" she asked, transforming into bitch mode.

Shawnee sensed Elaine's temper coming. "Look, Elaine, we've been doing the same jazz club for a little over a year now, and to be frank with you, I'm getting bored with going week after week. I would…actually, we all would like to switch things up from time to time. A jazz club is nice, but we don't have to do the same jazz club. We could also do movies, sporting events—something other than the same thing week after week."

"So, Shawnee, what exactly did you have in mind? You know I like to be there to hear Russell play. I want to be supportive of my man and don't need the headache of having to choose between my man and my sisters," Elaine snapped.

"You know, I really don't need any drama about this. Girls' night out is not just about Elaine. That's downright selfish of you to feel all of our lives are supposed to revolve around you and Russell. You can support your man on your own time and not have us roped into it with you. As for this Wednesday, we have decided to go to a party at the Megaplex. It wouldn't feel right without you, so hopefully, we won't be without you."

"Did I hear you say a party at the Megaplex? Why would I want to go hang out at some ghetto party at the Megaplex?" Elaine raised her voice. "Shawnee, I can't believe your married behind would even consider something like that. Worse than that, don't you think you're a little too old to be trying to party with a bunch of hoochies? Are you really that lonely?"

Elaine hit a nerve with Shawnee. She managed to take information Shawnee had shared and stabbed her in the heart with it.

"Elaine, you have hit a new low. I think I'm now done with this conversation. We will be at the Megaplex Wednesday. I'll email you the info. If we see you, we'll see you. Goodbye!" Shawnee slammed the phone down.

It shouldn't have come as a big surprise, because Elaine had always been a self-centered, over-the-top bitch. Shawnee thought for certain that Elaine would someday outgrow her ugly ways, but at twenty-nine, she seemed to be getting worse.

When their mother died of ovarian cancer two years ago, Elaine felt it wasn't her place to help pay for the funeral expenses because their mother, whom she always feuded with, should have taken more responsible measures in preparing for her imminent death. Of course, that thought went out the window when she learned their mother left each of her seven children a $100,000 life insurance policy, as well as provisions for her burial. Since Elaine had tied all of her inheritance up in her snobby shoe *boutique* in Georgetown, her attitude had become worse. Truth be known, the shoes were to die for and had prices starting at three hundred dollars. Fortunately for her, business had been very good. Unfortunately for all those around her, she'd become unbearable.

Ironically, Harmony lived up to her name and was the opposite of Elaine. Out of all the Wiggins' girls, Harmony was the most grounded and definitely the most reliable. She was always the peacemaker and the voice of reason. Sadly enough, she devoted so much of herself to her family and work that she made no time for herself. Along with her mother, she practically raised Sandy's children while working her way through college. Somehow, she managed to successfully achieve her doctorate in Psychology at Johns Hopkins University, while it took six years for Sandy to only get her Associate's in Accounting. Sandy would always make the excuse that she couldn't get any further because she had children to raise. Besides Angelo, who was nineteen years old and two years from completing his Bachelor's in Business, Sandy was the only one who didn't achieve her Bachelor's.

Now at thirty-three, with her shotgun-marriage to Lewis, Sandy's new career would more likely be keeping up with his philandering ways. She married Lewis in record time. About two weeks after meeting, Lewis was moving in with her and her children, and about another month or two later, they were having an economy wedding at the clubhouse in the community where they lived. Sandy was afforded the ability to live in a pretty decent community from the combination of her $30,000 yearly salary as an accounting clerk and her three separate child support cases, which provided generously for her two sons and one daughter.

Foolishly, Sandy packed her family up to move to Colorado to keep Lewis from constantly hitting on Charise and sometimes Elaine. Not just her sisters, she wanted Lewis to be far away from the mothers of

Lewis' other children. Somehow, she figured her life would be more peaceful. Although she'd only been in Denver for three months, she barely called any of her sisters, which was probably because she didn't want to have to tell anyone the grass wasn't greener in Denver after all.

The relationship between the Wiggins sisters had oftentimes been a tumultuous one, which caused the women to drift apart in their adult lives. Growing up in the rougher parts of D.C. would promote family unity when it came to having to do battle with other neighborhood girls. Their mother, having been the product of a large family raised in the rough areas of Detroit, would often incite fights in the neighborhood and drag her six daughters in the midst.

The Wiggins family lived in their own house versus living in the nearby projects, and the children were brought up to believe they were a "classy" bunch compared to those who were in the projects or on welfare. Although the household contained two working parents, most of the time making ends meet was a challenge because of the number of children and because their father often lost his jobs greatly due to his drinking. The challenge became even greater when he died fifteen years ago, leaving their mother working as a nurse to make it on her own with the remaining small children.

Their father, being a full-blooded Native American out of North Carolina, provided the girls with hair that grew far down their backs. However, that long hair was also another source of the many fights the girls experienced growing up. So much so, Shawnee kept her hair cut short ever since leaving home twenty years ago, greatly disappointing her mother.

A significant age difference also created a wedge between the sisters. That along with strong personalities, independent lifestyles, and the parents choosing favorites that bred hatred. Upon the death of Wilhelmina, thirteen years after the death of her husband, the sisters agreed to meet once a week in an effort to restore their bond, which barely existed growing up. Each Wednesday for the past two years, they had been getting together for their girls' night out. It started with the women gathering at either Harmony or Shawnee's house, but eventually changed into going out on the town for dinner and live music, ultimately getting stuck on the one jazz club.

The music was pumping with a nice R&B mixture at the Megaplex. The place was a converted warehouse. At only 6:30 p.m., there had to be at least three hundred women there. As the sisters looked around for a table, they spotted Elaine and her childhood friend, Renee, across the large club.

"Shawnee, I thought you said Elaine probably wouldn't show tonight?" Kelly asked, while laughing. "It looks like she beat us here."

"Well, she talked so much trash about how this place was ghetto, how there were nothing but hoochies, and me being too old. Of course, that left me to believe she wasn't going to show. Also, since no one heard from her since that conversation, I assumed she gave us her ass to kiss," Shawnee replied.

With hand on hip, Charise asked, "Can someone explain to me why she brought Renee along? I can't stand that bitch. Our girls' night out is for the Wiggins sisters only."

Shawnee answered, "I'm with you on that, lil' sis. Out of all the people she could have found, she would pick the one even Harmony doesn't like."

"I'm like shocked here," Harmony responded, while shaking her head. "I think Renee is the only person on earth whose attitude is worse than Elaine's. Every time she opens her mouth with that 'Well, Harmony, you're supposed to be so smart' nonsense, I want to punch her in it. The self-righteous bitch!"

The ladies all laughed at Harmony's sharp words and her imitation of Renee.

"Well, the way I see it, they came on their own. Neither of them told us they'd be here. So, I say let's just find our own separate table and not intrude upon them," Charise suggested. "She probably brought that bitch to spite us anyhow."

"Isn't that the truth?" Harmony agreed. "Sounds like a plan, Charise. I came to cut loose and have a good time. She's not going to spoil our night."

"Now you know that's not right," Kelly responded.

"Well, you go sit with them," Shawnee spat back to Kelly.

"I don't think so!" Kelly answered, and they all laughed. "And whatever you do, Harmony, don't start dancing."

"Girly, what are you talking about? I've been watching some of those videos and practicing for tonight. Shoot, I can do the Stanky Leg, the Jerk, the Dougie, even the Tootsie Roll," Harmony said, while slightly demonstrating.

"AW HELL NO! Harmony, if you don't cut that shit out, I'm gonna send your ass over there with your sister and her friend," Shawnee said as they continued to laugh. "How embarrassing."

Charise added, "And she's extra tall and stands out like a sore thumb."

"Everyone is tall to you Charise. Me and Harmony are only 5'10" compared to your short 5'3" behind," Shawnee joked.

"It's still embarrassing…both of you."

"I don't know what you're talking about. I got plenty of rhythm in these hips." Shawnee started swaying seductively to the beat.

"Eew! Stop! You remind me of Momma trying to be hip and dance," Charise laughed.

"Then you need to take lessons, kid," Harmony answered.

"Trust me, no one needs to give Charise lessons on being nasty. She can probably teach all of us a thing or two from the shit she tells me," Kelly shared.

The ladies made their way through the crowd in search of a table far away and out of sight from their sister and her incorrigible friend. Once seated, they quickly ordered Apple Martinis while they were still 2-for-1 priced. They ordered fourteen in all, although it was only four of them.

Three drinks later, the music stopped, lights lowered, a spotlight shined on the stage, and out came the evening's announcer. The announcer turned out to be a comedian. He had plenty of jokes, but it was a sore sight to look at him. Before announcing the first dancer, he had the nerve to joke about some of the women in the audience being fat, ugly, and probably having the biggest pocketbooks stuffed with the most dollar bills. Although what he said was funny as hell to the women, his short, roly-poly, ugly behind had no room to talk. Maybe coming from his mouth is what made the joke so funny. It could have been the 2-for-1 Apple Martinis. Nonetheless, it seemed like every woman in the place quickly sobered up when the first dancer, Meatloaf, stepped on the stage.

As the clothes peeled away, it became more obvious where his name Meatloaf came from. While every woman in Megaplex stood screaming to the top of their lungs, the Wiggins sisters stood in utter shock. Not that they had lived a sheltered life, but nothing had prepared them for a Meatloaf. It just didn't seem humanly possible to have such a construction.

"Oh my Lord!" Shawnee exclaimed. "How on earth could that be?" Then she let out a loud yell. "WHOOO! Over here, baby!" she said, holding a ten-dollar bill in the air.

"My sister has been turned out," Kelly laughed. "Would you look at that body? I am perspiring. I can't believe this."

Just then, Meatloaf gyrated his way over to collect Shawnee's money. He then took her hand and ran it over the front of his body, including his package of meatloaf. When Shawnee's hand actually made contact with his package, she acted virgin-like, pretending to almost faint. By this time, the Wiggins sisters joined in with the fondling while adding their own dollars to his g-string.

When the ladies regained their composure, Charise said, "I think the strip shows usually save their best for last."

Harmony answered, "I can't imagine anything topping this one."

Then the roly-poly announcer returned to the stage making a few jokes that probably no one was coherent enough to comprehend. All around the club, women were fanning themselves. It seemed as though the air conditioning went out. Now that Meatloaf had disappeared behind the curtain, the women were trying to recompose in hopes of feeling some air again. However, that air would be short lived when King Cobra appeared on stage. It didn't help matters that he entered by gyrating on the floor like a snake. After King Cobra came Foot Long and then Black Panther. After him came Rod-Knee, who bragged a member that wasn't too far off from his knees, which hardly reached down to the thick of his thigh.

Now, there was Meatloaf, King Cobra, Foot Long, Black Panther and Rod-Knee, each with rippling muscles and bodies to kill for. How could they possibly top what had already come?

First, the comedian had to come out to say his few insulting jokes, while giving the women an opportunity to recompose themselves. Then the comedian walked off the stage, saying it was not big enough to be on when the next guy came out. From behind the curtain, he also told the audience that he didn't want to be on stage when the next guy came and set it on fire. All lights went off, the club grew quiet, and sounds of the jungle started to play through the speakers.

"Ladies, let's give it up literally…" the comedian announced, pausing to laugh at his own joke, "for Mandingo."

A thunderous applause erupted, while still in the dark and not yet seeing Mandingo. Finally, a purple spotlight appeared upon what looked like a giant who was synchronizing with the onset of the music. Some women actually fainted at the sight of Mandingo, who stood 6'8". When the other lights came up, those who managed to find breath were able to scream. Others stood in shock and watched Mandingo go to work.

Upon the sight of Mandingo, Shawnee had to take a seat. As if on instinct, Mandingo made his way to Shawnee and started working her over. He began licking her breast with her clothes on. She didn't have an ounce of strength to put up a resistance as he buried his face underneath her skirt. The Wiggins sisters could only helplessly look on in shock, along with every other woman in the club, which totaled about six hundred by then. Shawnee never believed some strange man, who was not her husband, would publicly give her pleasure for the entire world to see. Hell, her husband would never be so uninhibited. Even more gracious of Mandingo, he left her with an orgasm that she'd reflect on for many days to come.

As Mandingo worked his way through the crowd, and Shawnee tried to collect herself, she heard an annoyingly familiar voice say, "Aren't you supposed to be married? Does that not count for anything anymore?"

Completely disturbed, she turned to see Renee standing disgruntled with her hands on her hips. While all the women in Megaplex were focused on Mandingo, Renee decided to focus on how to make yet another Wiggins sister miserable.

"You should be glad I left my camera phone on the table with

Elaine. Otherwise, I'd send you an email of your own despicable behavior," Renee bitterly added.

Having heard Renee's last comment and full of Apple Martinis, Harmony said, "You know, Renee, I really don't like your bitter behind, and that's not an easy task. Why Elaine insists on bringing you around all of us, who do not like you, is a mystery to us."

"Harmony, I can't believe you're saying these things to me," Renee retorted as if she were genuinely shocked and had no knowledge that the Wiggins sisters despised her.

Harmony cut her off, slurring, "Well, believe it!"

"But it sounds as though you're condoning this type of behavior from a married woman, and I would think with all of your education, you should know better." Renee tried to defend her by asking, "Are you inebriated, Harmony?"

Charise, who was also full of drinks, mistakenly picked up on what Renee had said to Harmony. "Ain't nobody deviated, bitch! Always trying to use big words and don't even know what they mean. When ya ugly ass gonna realize you will never be a Wiggins sister no matter how hard you try? Since you were a kid, you been trying to be a Wiggins, calling our mother 'Momma Wiggins.' You need to get the hell away from our family, because this night is about us, the Wiggins sisters," she said, pointing to herself and her sisters who were watching. "And last I checked, you weren't one of us. That's why yo' momma ran off and left your ugly ass for the garbage man. She didn't want you either."

The sisters cackled at Charise's words.

Renee gasped. "Well! I don't need to take this abuse from you all." Then she disappeared into the crowd as Mandingo disappeared behind the curtains.

"Dang, she made me miss the rest of Mandingo's act. I should go belt her in the mouth for that, plus for once again telling me how educated I am supposed to be," Harmony angrily stated.

Kelly came over to the girls screaming and all hyped up. She had followed Mandingo around the club, feeling him up every chance she could get. "Whew! Woo Hoo!" she shouted before noticing the looks of anger on her sisters' faces. "Okay, what did I miss?"

"Renee," Shawnee answered.

"Enough said. I ran into uptight Elaine on the other side, getting her freak on with Mandingo. He practically had her bare boob in his mouth, and she didn't give a damn that I was watching. I also think he had his hand under her skirt, by the look on her face," Kelly shared.

"So while Renee was over here trying to be Miss Righteous, she missed her friend being publicly freaked?" Harmony asked before erupting into laughter.

Shawnee felt a twinge of jealousy by Kelly's words. After all, Mandingo had just finished making her feel good. She tried to laugh to keep her feelings hidden.

Just then, Elaine made her way over, smiling and saying, "Sisters, what's up? I saved a table for us on the other side when I arrived. I can't believe you all were here this entire time. Let me go get Renee so we can come over here."

"I'm sorry, sister, but we will not be tolerating Renee tonight," Shawnee answered stoically.

Elaine looked confused. "I don't understand. Renee has been my friend forever. What's the problem?"

Shawnee answered, "Elaine, Renee is your friend, and every time she comes around she manages to insult each and every one of us. We don't want the nonsense tonight, especially on our night. If you can ditch the witch, then we'd love for you to join us. If not, then keep that walking disaster on the other side of the club with her ashy, crater face."

"Wow! I'm shocked. First, I have to choose between my sisters and my man. When I choose my sisters, now they are making me choose between my friend and them. I gotta draw the line on that one. I'll see you guys later," Elaine said before walking away.

"Okay, that went well," Harmony said.

"Elaine is always going to be Elaine," Kelly responded. "Maybe the more she cuts herself off, the clearer she will be able to see the world for what it truly is."

"You might have a point there, sis. Elaine has always had us to have her back or be her sounding board," Harmony replied.

Charise added, "Whipping board is more like it."

The girls shared a laugh.

"Now, can we get back to enjoying our evening?" Charise asked the others.

"Sounds good to me," Shawnee chimed in, holding her glass up for a toast.

The ladies all joined their glasses together.

PART ONE

After the Party

1

Shawnee

Hello, I'm Shawnee Clarise Wiggins-Townsend. I am the 38-year-old eldest child of Wilhelmina and Henry Wiggins. Despite being the eldest, I haven't always been the shining example for my younger siblings. I've always enjoyed a free spirit and have balanced the things I had to do in life with the things I want to do.

Since my childhood, I have always been very creative and outgoing. I knew early on that I wanted to work in an industry that would allow me to creatively express myself, while making plenty of money. As a result, I am now a senior partner for an advertising company, The Right Look, Inc.

I didn't have much difficulty climbing the corporate ladder because I was always driven. Having the right physical assets also contributed to my success. I know this may sound sexist, but when I knew I was up against a man or another woman for a promotion, or even grabbing clients, I would tastefully reveal just enough cleavage or thigh to generate the creative juices in the minds of the persons I was trying to sell. My boss and owner of the company, Mr. Neely, is an older white man who loves flying into town just to catch a glimpse of whatever I let be seen, and I have yet for him to refuse me anything I want. However, the company always fares well as a result of my creative control, and Mr. Neely is very happy about that. Shawnee Wiggins would never let a deal get away. Oh no, not in this lifetime. Hell, I can turn women on, as well, without ever crossing the line. Men are like putty in my hands. My very competitive nature has driven me to do things that would cause my momma to roll over in her grave. I would say Daddy, too, but he stayed too drunk to really give a shit.

One of my other childhood goals was to marry a lawyer or doctor. I managed to snag Robert, who is a well-paid corporate attorney. To top that, he is definitely what one would call eye candy—on the nerdy side but definitely eye candy. Thankfully, he's nothing like the dog Sandy married. No need for a leash with Robert. We actually dated for a year and a half before he proposed marriage. Robert is one of those romantic types who like to do things big. So, while attending a Washington Wizards game, he made a public proposal for the world to see. At the time, I still had a wild streak in me, so marriage wasn't high on my priority list. But, when someone publicly proposes, how can you shoot them down? A year and a half later, I became Mrs. Townsend. During our four years of marriage, I have been completely faithful to Robert. Maybe a bit on the flirty side, but never crossed the line.

Robert knew I was a highly sexual woman when he first met me. What he lacked in sexuality, he made up in romancing. The heavy romancing would be enough to guilt me into always being faithful. Duracell compensated for the sexual differences. As of late, Robert has been on this excessive working kick. As a result, the minimal amount of sex has almost diminished to non-existent. Even worse, the romancing is vanishing. I'm sitting here becoming afraid of getting battery-acid poisoning. That's how many batteries I've been through lately.

It is my opinion it's Robert's fault that Mandingo had the opportunity to have his way with me after we left Megaplex on

Wednesday. Little did my sisters know, while Mandingo was underneath my skirt doing his thing, he managed to slip a piece of paper inside my thong that read, *Call me: 202-555-1374*. I didn't know it was there until I went to the ladies' room. I kept feeling something irritating after he played inside my pussy, but I thought he must have scratched me. I was just glad he was in my pussy first before touching the other girls. When I dug the wet piece of paper out of me, my first thought was to throw it away, but when I reflected back on the orgasm I had just received in the club, I thought differently. I wondered how many of those women that he was servicing in the club had he slipped his number to. I also wondered if he slipped his number to Elaine, as well. The thought of her getting him instead of me just didn't sit well with me; I couldn't chance it.

I was anxious to get away from my sisters to call Mr. Mandingo and see what else he had to offer. So, I decided to bail on them at 10:30 that night. As Mandingo made his rounds after the show, he spent most of his time making eye contact with me wherever he moved. It could have been my imagination that he was watching me, but since we were peeling off clothes at the Sheraton by 11:15 p.m., it would be safe to say it wasn't my imagination. Mandingo showed me erogenous zones on my body I didn't know existed. The way he kissed my body had me tingling all over. That night, I also learned I could actually take twelve inches through the back door. I've had twelve inches in the front door before, but never the back. Once upon a time, I enjoyed anal sex, but Robert was a turn off in that department. So, we gave up that part of our sex life. Thankfully, I had my erotic toys to supplement. But, after having twelve inches of Mandingo in my ass, my toys might get the boot. As for Robert, he can keep working those late hours until his heart's content.

I made it home by 1:45 that morning, and I was on cloud nine. I got a bit turned on by the thought of being with two men back to back.

There were a few past occasions when I was with two at a time. That was ages ago, so now I could only settle for a back-to-back sex session.

When I climbed into bed with Robert, he tried to play sleep. I knew he wasn't, though. I decided to fondle him and seductively wake him up, but the bastard had the nerve to blow me off with a "not tonight, honey. I have to get up early in the morning."

That next morning, I went to work still fuming by the continuous rejection. However, that all changed when my secretary told me there was a Mr. Bradshaw on the line. I wondered who that could be, but was unable to figure it out.

"Shawnee Wiggins here," I answered. Okay, so I wouldn't change my last name at work.

"Hey, sexy," some delicious sounding specimen said on the other end. "Do you have plans for lunch today?"

I sat there a bit confused. *Who is this inquiring about my lunch plans?* I did give my work number to Mandingo, but during our lack of conversation, I didn't bother asking his real name. His voice sounded so much sexier than what I remembered from the night before.

"I'm sorry, but who am I speaking with?"

"This would be Eric Bradshaw, also known as Mandingo," he responded. "I didn't think it was appropriate to call your job identifying myself as Mandingo."

I felt an immediate throbbing sensation between my legs, while my nipples stood at attention as if trying to tell me how to respond to his question.

"Well, Mr. Bradshaw, I'm sure I can make some adjustments in my schedule. What did you have in mind?" I anxiously answered.

His sexiness responded, "I was hoping you would be able to swing by my loft for the lunch I will prepare for you. I thought I'd also massage out any tension that the morning may have caused. Your office is near my loft."

OH MY LORD! Please help me put up some resistance here.

"Okay," I answered without the hesitation I would like to have given. "What time would you like to see me?"

"I would like to see you now, but I know you have to get some work done, and I still need to prepare your lunch," he replied. "I will leave it to your discretion, Miss Wiggins."

"Give me the address, and let's plan on around one," I said.

"Sounds good." Then he gave me the address before we hung up.

Now, the typical rule for a one-night stand is to take no prisoners and don't exchange numbers, but between the Apple Martinis and his extra large dick up in me, I forgot all the rules, including the one about cheating on your husband.

For the rest of the morning, I couldn't concentrate on anything else. My ass still had a sensual soreness from the previous night, but I was certainly looking forward to round two completely sober. Mr. Bradshaw had certainly met his match when it comes to freaky. Some things a woman just never outgrows, but perfects instead.

My sensual thoughts were intruded upon when my secretary buzzed me to let me know Robert was on the phone.

"Hi, Robert," I answered, trying to sound like I gave a hoot.

"Hey, baby. How's your day going?" he asked like he really gave a damn.

"Just another day, Robert. Just another day." This time, I let him hear the attitude.

"Shawnee, I know you're getting tired of my excessive work hours and lack of affection, but I promise all that will be fixed," he answered. "As a matter of fact, how about I pick you up for lunch today?"

Is this man stupid or what?! He thinks he's going to make up a lack of intimacy with a fucking lunch? For Robert, lunch is just that: lunch. You don't know how many times I fell for the okie-doke, thinking he would someday get a clue when it came to "lunch". I went as far as suggesting to him, as Harmony advised me to, that we combine lunches with intimacy. Needless to say, I was shot down because he felt it wasn't cool to go back in the office smelling of sex.

"Sorry, Robert, I have a project we're working on. Maybe we could grab dinner tonight?" I lied.

"Ooh, sorry. That won't work. I have a client to meet for dinner, and I know you can't stand sitting in on my client dinners," he answered.

He got that shit right! Typically, his male clients spent most of the dinner checking out my boobs while I'm sitting and my ass when I stand. I won't lie, I liked the attention, but it's always a source for mine and Robert's arguments. When he has women clients, he basically shows off and is the king of flirt. I'm not supposed to complain about that, though, because I'm supposed to know "it's only business".

"Well, I guess I'll see you at home tonight whenever you get there," I responded in the most unenthusiastic voice.

"I hope you have on something sexy when I get home, because we have some lost time to make up," he said, trying to sound seductive.

I ought to wear flannel pajamas tonight in mid-June. Suddenly, I perked up when I thought of getting that back-to-back sex I missed the night before.

"I'm looking forward to it, Robert."

"I won't let you down, Shawnee," he answered.

After hanging up, all concentration went out the window, literally. I spent the rest of the morning gazing out of the windows of my large corner office that I obtained after seducing Mr. Neely. My mind created every fantasy it could imagine, with the king-sized chocolate Mandingo being the star. The more I thought, the more aroused I became. I was half tempted to whip out my portable bullet that I keep in my purse for whenever the urge hits, but I decided to hold out. The only thing to do at this point was to wait until one o'clock. As I waited, I wondered why the name Eric Bradshaw sounded so familiar to me. I can't say we have met before. I'm sure I would never forget meeting a man of his size. I also can't remember anyone I knew dating someone with that name.

Oh well, I won't give it any more thought until I return from "lunch". Then I will call Harmony to see if the name is familiar to her.

I was greeted at the elevator with a single pink rose and Mandingo wearing black silk boxers and a black silk robe that exposed his smooth, bare chest. I also was greeted by the aroma of Cajun spices cooking. The kiss he planted on my lips continued from the doorway into the loft and until I was stripped down to my bare skin. Mandingo licked me from head to toe, frontwards and backwards. I returned the favor before he planted his 12-inch, or maybe longer, train into my excessively wet train station.

Damn, I hadn't noticed the night before, but his dick looks bigger. More intimidating this time. Whew! But it feels sensational.

It was probably an hour later before I got to taste his deliciously prepared gumbo. After the next round, which included the anal penetration I had so longed for, he pampered me with a sensual full body massage. I grabbed a quick wash before skipping my happy-go-lucky behind back to work with some of the gumbo and a sore ass.

Once in my office, I shuffled around a few papers, but couldn't think about anything except for part two with Robert. My thought of the name Eric Bradshaw did return to mind, so I called my non-judgmental sister Harmony to share my deeds with.

Have to tell somebody. Also, she may know the name.

"Eric Bradshaw is the guy Sandy was messing around with a few years back," she informed me after my asking.

"Did you ever meet him? Do you know what he looks like?" I asked on the verge of panic, hoping it wasn't one and the same.

"I haven't personally met him. I know Elaine met him. Also, I know he supposedly has a massive-sized penis. That part Sandy couldn't stop talking about," answered Harmony.

"Oh boy, not good," I sulked. "By any chance, do you know where he lives?"

"All I know is that he had a loft somewhere downtown, I think. I believe he was someone she knew from high school," Harmony added, then paused before shouting into the phone, "Shawnee! What have you done? How well do you know this Eric Bradshaw?"

I cringed as my stomach turned in disgust of having slept with one of my sister's boyfriends.

"In the biblical sense," I confessed.

"Shawnee, have things gotten that bad between you and Robert? How did this happen, and how long has it been going on?" Harmony asked.

"Harmony, Eric Bradshaw is Mandingo, and it began after I left you guys last night," I answered, embarrassed.

"Girl, I am disappointed, but I'm not mad at you!" she laughed. "What are you going to do?"

"I don't know. We're supposed to hook up tomorrow for quote, unquote *lunch*. To answer your question about Robert and me, our sex life has deteriorated to hell. We actually have an appointment for tonight. Would you believe that? An appointment! Last night, he rejected my advances. It's been almost three weeks, Harmony," I pleaded.

"You don't have to explain to me. I know you've been trying everything you can to get his attention. I just don't want you to get hurt, being caught up in a triangle," Harmony advised.

"I'll play it safe. Lord knows I would hate for this to get back to Elaine or Sandy," I said before another thought crossed my mind. "Wait a minute! Didn't you say Elaine already met him?"

Harmony answered, "Yeah, I think it was three or four years ago."

"I just remembered. Didn't Kelly come back to the table last night talking about Mandingo practically had Elaine's tit in his mouth?" I asked.

"I think I do remember that. Ooh, that's not cool at all," Harmony said.

"That means Elaine knew who Mandingo was while she was plopping her tit in his mouth," I stated. "That's trifling."

"Well, you knew he had his mouth on her tits when you decided to give him some of your goodies," Harmony said, trying to be the eternal voice of reason.

"I gave him the benefit of the doubt since we weren't sitting together and he didn't know we were together," I defended.

"Eeeww! You all are nasty," she laughed. "I guess that logic works for a married woman."

"And it was damn good. Worth all the tea in China," I laughed back. "Like I said earlier, I would like this to stay between you and me."

Harmony played confused. "What? I don't know what you're talking about."

"Thank you, sis," I said, getting serious.

"Just be careful, girl. You know I'll always have your back," Harmony responded.

We talked a bit more before ending the call.

That night when Robert got home at 12:30 a.m., he went straight to sleep without giving what he promised because he had an early morning meeting.

2
Elaine

Being the middle child has always been a struggle for me. Daddy was the only one who paid me any attention, and Momma resented him and me for it. She was probably happy when he died just so I wouldn't get any more attention.

We all had long hair while growing up, and the witch never wanted to fix my hair. However, she would let Sandy and Harmony take turns experimenting in my hair, while she always kept their hair perfect. Shawnee was just too perfect to have to ever fix my hair. No one experimented in Kelly's hair. That was Momma's other saint 'cause she'd tell every damn thing. However, my daddy would take only me to the beauty shop so I could be his princess, and Momma hated that.

I have always been the more vocal one in the family, but it seems like no matter what I say, no one ever listens to what I think or feel. Talk about feeling like Jan Brady of the *Brady Bunch*. That would be the story of my life. My family feels I'm spoiled and materialistic. They don't realize I had to fight for everything I have. If I'm spoiled, it's because I had to spoil my damn self.

My daddy died of some kind of sudden liver failure supposedly as a result of alcohol when I was fourteen years old. Then I simply fell between the cracks in the Wiggins household. I always aspired to be rich and famous, just like my daddy told me I could be. I spent most of my life living in a fantasy world. I rationalized everything in my mind and could convince others quite easily since I was convinced myself.

By the age of sixteen, I had many boyfriends. Okay, well maybe they were only sex partners. Nonetheless, the attention helped fill the void left in me by Daddy's death. By the age of seventeen, I made all of my "boyfriends" my tricks. Yeah, they had to start paying for this pussy, and they didn't have any problems with it. At eighteen, I was buying my own damn car, and I also stepped up the financial contributions of my "tricks." I figured a Georgetown University education wasn't going to come cheap, and I hardly had my momma to turn to for guidance and support. She was too busy funneling her monies into Angelo, Sandy's babies, and Harmony and Shawnee's education.

Most mothers would have been proud to have a child attending Georgetown University. Not mine. Kelly attending Howard was a bigger deal than me attending Georgetown. The fact that I graduated in three years didn't even make her ass proud of me. Bitch didn't even attend my graduation. All of her family came in from Detroit, and she didn't show up nor offer any explanation or congratulations. Ironically, she always referred to me as a whore, not knowing what I did for a living, and her only words to my sisters were, "I'm surprised the whore had it in her to keep her legs closed long enough to get an education."

My new tricks would be professional men. Race, age, or nationality was not a factor. I can say I was doing quite well for myself. I was constantly lavished with expensive gifts, and by my junior year in college, this politician put me up in a plush apartment. Another of my tricks upgraded my Toyota Camry to a BMW, minus the headache of a car note. The one who got my apartment only requested that I not bring any other guys in the place. I had no problem giving him that respect since I particularly enjoyed going to posh hotels around the world. Yes, I said around the world. I've been flown to Paris, Morocco, Japan, French Riviera, Fiji Islands, Brazil, and various Caribbean islands. Domestically, I've been flown to Los Angeles, Seattle, Phoenix, Las Vegas, Atlanta, New York, and Denver. All of this from hooking.

Since I had long ago fell between the cracks in the Wiggins household, no one really paid any attention to the fact that I had yet to graduate from college and was already living large. Eventually, Sandy caught on and would blackmail me with her newfound info. But, soon, I had her turned out and turning tricks, as well. Sandy certainly wasn't in a position to offer me any big sister guidance, so she fell in line. Sandy didn't make a good hooker because she was too emotional and always looking for love from a trick. It didn't help that she already had three children, and it showed on her body. Me, I have a body to die for. I have a body that even turns the heads of women. Speaking of which, I don't discriminate. I'll get with women, too, for the right price.

My body is something I take great pride in. It is my biggest asset— my money-maker. I do Yoga, Tai-Chi, and kickboxing, as well as running to keep this perfect figure. I have been fortunate that my boobs have no need for a bra other than for my workouts. I like to call them great conversation pieces. I love the hypnotic effect they have on men, especially when my nipples are hard or I happen to be wearing a fitted t-shirt (designer, of course). These boobies yield me new tricks every day, not to mention the power-ass I carry. Like I said, a body to die for. No flab, no gut. Hell, I get turned on looking at my own self in the mirror, with or without clothes. Some tricks pay me just so they can look at my body. They may touch it as if it was a precious jewel, but they don't want to violate it with sex. And I know for a fact that my sisters hate that I have the best body of the family. They probably wish they could be me and have what I have.

By the time I graduated college, I was the proud owner of a two-bedroom condo not too far from the White House. I took a piece of job to look completely legit, but I wasn't giving up my true bread and butter.

Momma's death two years ago yielded me one hundred thousand dollars, which I really didn't need. However, it provided the front I needed to open my shoe boutique in Georgetown. Anyone with any real sense would know it should have taken more than $100k to open that boutique, but I just say it's a down payment. I sell expensive women's shoes —the kind that I would wear. I get many celebrities coming through the door. Additionally, I get many wealthy men who come to shop for their women. About sixty percent of them turn out to be one of my tricks. Hell, I'm trying to open a string of boutiques. A girl's gotta do what a girl's gotta do.

Although Momma's death barely moved me, my sisters were deeply affected by it. Somehow, we eventually started doing girls' night out every Wednesday. Because everyone kinda went their own separate ways after becoming grown, we acted like we all lived in different states right in Maryland and D.C. Charise and Kelly have their little clique; Shawnee and Harmony have theirs. Sandy and I just fit in wherever, whenever. During girls' night out, Sandy met Lewis, fell in love, and married that loser in record time. She had to have known that he tried to get with me and Charise. She never knew he had actually been with Renee, who is another story I'll get back to.

We started hanging at this jazz club, which is where I found Russell. I'm not an emotional creature, but somehow, his saxophone had me wetting my panties. I think he knew he got me when I started fanning myself. Then each week that we'd go there, he would make me his target. It took about three months of courting before Russell caught a whiff of this pussy. And I mean that literally. He actually begged to at least smell it. So, I let him do just that. Maybe a month or so later, I finally gave him some—the first free pussy I had given away since the age of seventeen. My nose is wide open, but not so much that I'm going to put Russell before a trick who wants to pay me.

Russell is broke and lacks ambition. He's content with staying as a headliner in that jazz club forever. In reality, the only real time I make for Russell is when we go there on Wednesdays and an occasional Sunday when no one else is on schedule. I can't really see myself settling with him because he can't provide me the lifestyle I have become accustomed to, but I do like the attention he gives me. He adores the ground I walk on and doesn't question my lack of availability to him. It also feels good having a man that I can call my own, although he has never stepped foot in my home. Of course, his primary purpose in my life is to keep my family off of my ass about why I never have a man.

One thing I don't do is bring a man up into my home. First, if Russell would see the very valuable items I have in my home, he'd start seeing dollar signs. Secondly, I don't need his ass snooping around and finding shit he doesn't need to see or know about. When I want to see him, I go to his place. That keeps me from getting too attached to his broke ass.

Renee is my closest friend. I've known her since middle school. I used to think she just hung around to be a part of my family. That's definitely what my sisters feel. After my dad passed, I somewhat pulled away from her, but you could still find her at the dinner table. She also helped manage my hair when my sisters didn't want to be bothered. When we were both sixteen and giving away plenty of free pussy, we were the closest ever. Renee never got away from giving free pussy away, though. When I suggested making guys pay for it, you would have sworn her judgmental behind was a preacher's daughter. So, I left her to her own devices. While in college, she noticed I was living a bit extravagantly and questioned if I was prostituting my body. I told her that I was dating this Sugar Daddy who wanted to take care of me. She never questioned my lifestyle again.

Okay, the story with Renee and Lewis: She and I went to a different jazz spot one night, and while all the men were tripping over me, she was tripping over herself to get to Lewis, who we hadn't known at the time. Don't get me wrong, Lewis is fine as hell, but not my type. He's full of himself. Renee was buying his ass drinks all night and somehow ended up fucking him in her car that night.

The first night I ran into Lewis while with my sisters, he tried to holla at me, but I reminded him of his romp in the hay with Renee. He swore he never touched her and said if he actually did, it was because she had drugged him. I wasn't convinced, so he moved on to my sister who was willing to give him the time of day – Sandy. Charise kind of seemed like she wanted Lewis herself, but knew he was ten years older than her. So, she backed off. However, it didn't stop Lewis from flirting with her or trying to get with me every chance that Sandy turned her head. Then, before you knew it, Sandy was marrying his ass. She accused me of being jealous when I told her that he tried to get with me and Charise. Instead of kicking his ass to the curb, she moved to Denver with him. Dumb ass! And Renee is still sticking by her story about fucking Lewis first.

Renee was glad to see Russell in my life, because it gave her the impression that I'm on the straight and narrow. Little does she know, he asks me all the time how could I hang out with such an ugly woman. He also thinks she has a bad attitude. Now note, I did say she was my closest friend, but we are hardly close. I don't have her all up in my business. She's an underpaid social worker, still giving her pussy away for free to anyone who says the right thing to her ugly ass. The sad thing is with all the pussy she gives away, she can't even afford to buy a pair of shoes from my boutique. I did give her a four-hundred-dollar pair of sandals for one hundred dollars because she is supposed to be my friend and I felt sorry for her. I'm a business woman first and foremost, so I had to collect some monies.

However, tonight…tonight is going to be one of those "Free Pussy" nights. I know Eric used to be Sandy's man a few years back, but when I put my hand on his huge dick last night at Megaplex, I couldn't resist the temptation. It didn't help the way he licked my tits while not giving a damn who was looking. For a brief moment, it felt like there was no one else in the room. Thankfully, Renee had gone to the ladies' room when he made his stop. I did notice Kelly staring in my face, but I know she didn't see him slip his number under my skirt and inside my thong when his finger penetrated me. I thought I had died and gone to heaven just in that short moment. I also remember some of the erotic tales Sandy would share with me. My pussy would contract as she gave me the details. So, now, I'll get to see what all the hype was about.

I remember when I actually got to meet him. They were at Potomac Mills Mall. Everyone in the mall was staring at this large man, probably thinking he was a ball player of some sort. I was staring because I finally had a face to go with those erotic stories. Our meeting was brief since Sandy had to whisk him away from all the women who were blatantly flirting with her man, in her face.

When he first came out in the club, I didn't really get a good look at him, but when his tongue was tickling my nipple, I knew exactly who he was. Hey, what Sandy don't know won't hurt her. She didn't know about Renee and Lewis, and she doesn't have to know about me and Eric.

I arrived at 9:30 p.m. at his tastefully decorated loft. He said he was fixing lobster, and I smelled a mixture of food scents as I stepped off the elevator. In his doorway, he stood there dressed in jeans that looked like they were suffocating his package and a wifebeater. His feet were bare, and from beneath the material, his nipples protruded in a sensuous way that just called to be sucked on.

He greeted me with a gentle kiss on the lips and then said, "You look really familiar to me in the light. I'm generally good with faces, but your name doesn't ring a bell."

Do I dare let this man know before I get the dick that he was dating my sister and we met a few years back? I don't think so. Not before I get to sample the goods.

So I lied. "I'm sure I'd remember if we knew each other, and we don't." I switched to a seductive tone. "However, Gracie wants to get to know you."

"Who's Gracie?" he asked, confused.

After I pulled up my miniskirt and exposed my bare kitty kat, no other words were spoken. He lifted me up to his shoulders and started kissing Gracie hello. He carried me to the large sofa, laid me down, and went to town. No matter how much pushing away I did or trying to run after the second and third orgasm, he wouldn't let up. I finally convinced him to give my throbbing breasts some attention. While licking, fondling, groping, and sucking, we managed to come out of our clothes, with the exception of my white come-fuck-me sandals.

I gasped when I finally saw the thirteen or fourteen inches of his beautiful dick. Not only was it long, but it had some width to it, as well as unblemished. In the club, I thought I felt twelve inches, but this was a welcomed surprise. I damn sure don't give away free blowjobs, not even to Russell, but this one I couldn't resist.

I might get lip burned with this big boy, I thought.

Maybe I had something to prove, but I wasn't going to pass up the opportunity. One thing is for certain, if he ever recalled meeting me through Sandy, he wouldn't remember her fucking him half as well as I was about to put it on him. I was going to make sure he never forgot me again.

I took his massive member down my throat, deep into my pussy, and for the finale, way deep inside my ass (also another thing I don't give away for free). That's one thing I knew he couldn't get with

Sandy. She wasn't having anal sex for any man. I knew I would be tasting dick in my mouth from the anal sex, and my ass would be sore for at least a week, but oh, it felt so good. And when he was done fucking this ass, he went back to licking and kissing it. After my body lay lifeless, he finished me off with a full body massage. Hell, I was almost tempted to pay his ass for the service. That's how good that shit felt.

It was around midnight when I got that lobster. I think dinner would have probably tasted better if I would have eaten upon arrival, but I had worked up such an appetite that I left nothing on the plate but shells.

After round two, I was able to make it home at five o'clock in the morning. I have never spent that much time fucking one man. A couple of hours tops, and your time is up. It was probably a one-shot deal, but it was definitely the Eighth Wonder that needed to be experienced at least once in a lifetime by every woman.

I guess this is one of those secrets I need to take to my grave. I can't tell my sisters about it, and Renee is so…so…so Renee. I don't dare tell her. I need to find more friends. Nah…I'm too cute for them bitches.

3

Charise

Megaplex bore some pretty decent fruit. I got three phone numbers that night. I was glad Shawnee left early. It was almost like being in the club with your momma. However, I was a bit surprised by her lack of resistance when it came to Mandingo. After that, she was back to being Miss Straight & Narrow. As usual, Kelly was being her flirty self, and Shawnee was like a bug up her ass. Kelly defended her actions by saying it was just innocent flirtation and reminded Shawnee of her three-month rule. Then the bitch had the nerve to divert Shawnee's attention onto how seductively I was dancing. Shawnee left around 10:30 that night, and Harmony left not too long after her. Kelly was determined not to leave me alone in the club, so we were out by 11:30. I don't know if Elaine and Renee were still there. It got so packed in the club, finding anyone was almost impossible.

By midnight, I was home alone. Talk about pissed off. I whipped out my three phone numbers and decided whoever answered first would get the prize for the night. Arnold is such a boring name to me, but he was the first to answer. Now, he is gorgeous as I don't know what—6'2" with a lovely body and healthy-sized dick. Even smells good. However, he arrived by 1:00 a.m. and was put out by 2:00 a.m.

What a lame-ass fuck. Waste of a big dick is what he is. Damn, I could have had a V-8, or better yet, some sleep. He couldn't understand why he was being put out so soon. I couldn't understand why he thought he was doing something. He acted all anxious about eating my pussy and couldn't even bring me to an orgasm. When I got tired of him trying, I just let him put his dick in me. He reminded me of a dog in heat the way he was humping on me. Thankfully, that ordeal lasted all of two minutes. He had the nerve to be sweating. Worse, he asked if I had made it back from heaven yet. I was like, "Huh?!" That was grounds for him to leave. The fool actually thought he turned me out.

After he left, I whipped out one of my sex toys and used my dirty-ass brother-in-law as the subject of my sexual fantasy. Lewis used to make passes at me all the time. I knew his ass wanted me the first day he saw me, but my sisters weren't having it because he's ten years older than I.

At first, his passes were subtle, but then, he started getting bolder. It started with "accidentally" brushing against my ass or breast. Finally, one time while at their apartment, before they were married, Sandy was in the shower, and Lewis opened his robe to show me his bare, erect at least ten-inch dick. I was shocked. When I tried to get away, he followed me into the kitchen and pressed it up against me. Then his fingers made their way under my skirt and into my pantyhose and panties. He had my pussy so wet that I was embarrassed when his fingers found that wetness. He started sucking on my breast through my blouse. His fingers were going in and out of my pussy so skillfully that I almost sat on the counter to let him fully have his way. As he licked my ear and the nape of my neck, I fought moans from escaping. I wanted him deeper inside of me. I moved my hips, helping him go deeper. Then the water from the shower stopped, and his fingers disappeared from my dripping wet pussy, bringing me back to where I was and who I was with. He licked his fingers before washing his hands at the sink.

Trying to recompose myself, I rushed back into the living room before Sandy came out and saw us together. When I looked down at my blouse, I noticed a large wet spot around my hardened nipple. I picked up my cup that was on the coffee table and intentionally spilled the water on my blouse to disguise the wet spot. I could tell Sandy suspected something when she came out, but she pretended to laugh at the alleged mess I made on myself. I told her that I was going to have to run back home and change before we went to church. My excuse was my way out of the situation that day, and they were married not long after.

Lewis's fingers made it into my pussy at least three more times after that. My bare breast also made its way into his mouth on two of those occasions, and I managed to get a full-blown orgasm. I was wishing he'd quickly slip his big dick in me at least a couple of strokes. I needed to feel it inside of my pussy. I even wanted to suck it. I loved its feel in my hand. I guess I forgot to mention the one time he did get to lick the kitty and put his finger in my asshole. I know Sandy had to hear me briefly scream out, even with the shower running. After that, she blocked my coming to her house unless the kids were there to keep a watchful eye on things. Sandy was leaving absolutely no more opportunities for us to come into contact.

Lewis would call me quite often to phone fuck me. Yes, I said phone fuck. He would talk about how his big dick would be squeezed inside of my tight pussy, while his finger would be fucking me in my ass. He would talk about how he would suck all the juices out of my wet pussy. He would have me working my own body and sucking my own tits. The more he talked about it, the more I wanted it.

When Lewis started with the subtle passes, I did tell Sandy, but she just dismissed the actions as accidents. However, once I caught a glimpse of that dick and he touched the hot spot, mum was the word of the day.

Since they moved to Denver, Lewis still calls me when he can manage to steal a moment. He told me that he can't even fuck Sandy without thinking of me. Now I know that's some cruel shit, but it's flattering to my ego. So, I continue to pretend he is fucking me righteously. I get multiple orgasms each time I do. And after Arnold left, imaginary Lewis handled business.

I was awakened by the phone at 7:37 that following morning. My clock was set for 7:45. Not cool. The caller ID showed an unfamiliar number in the Denver area. I quickly came to life. As my pussy instincts would serve me, Lewis was on the other end.

"Hey girl, did I wake you?" he asked.

"Yeah, but I had to get up in a few. What is this number you're calling me from?" I asked.

"I picked up a throwaway cell. Sandy checks my cell phone bill, so I don't want to call you from that phone," he responded.

"You know I don't have time for any phone activity this morning, right?" I said. "You should have called at your normal time."

He chuckled before replying, "Well, actually, I'm calling to find out how interested you are in really having this big, black dick up in that tight pussy."

I almost choked. *Is this man serious or is this part of the phone sex game we play?*

"And how is that supposed to happen?" I asked. "How are you supposed to get free from the clutches of Sandy?"

"You don't worry your pretty head about that. I just need to know if you want me like I want your pussy in my mouth and on my hard dick," he responded.

At this point, my pussy was soaking wet.

I hesitantly answered, "Well, I guess so." Suddenly, boldness took over. "Does my ass get attention, also?"

"I don't know. How about you open your door and find out?" he said.

Now totally confused, I asked, "Huh? Open the door? My door?"

Just then, my doorbell rang while my alarm went off. I stumbled off the bed to stop the clock and then turned my attention back to the phone, but the line was dead. The doorbell rang again more persistently. I collected myself and ran to the door to look out the peephole.

Oh my goodness! Lewis is outside my door! Think! Think! I'm about to sleep with my sister's husband all the way if I open this door. I have on a gown with no panties. There's no resistance, no barriers.

The thought of the many times I wanted him inside of me overshadowed any sense of right and wrong.

The doorbell rang again, and the door was opened.

"Oh my goodness! Lewis! What are you doing here?" I asked.

"Can I come in, or do I have to stay here in the hallway?" he asked in return.

I stepped back to allow him to enter and hurried to close the door before Sandy's imaginary spies caught her husband coming into my apartment.

Lewis didn't say another word. He just picked me up, carried me to my sofa, and raised my gown that provided his mouth instant access to my pussy. Between his fingers and tongue working my pussy, I couldn't get out more than a moan. While his fingers were deeply embedded inside my pussy, he turned me over and began licking and nibbling on my ass. He then transferred his finger from inside my pussy to inside my ass. While he was doing that, he got his pants down to his ankles and plunged his bare licorice black dick into my hot, wet pussy. He had me practically upside down while he went in and out, and in and out, grinding his pelvis as far as my own pelvis would let him get in. I was biting the hell out of my sofa pillows to muffle my screams. Then he suddenly pulled out and finally spoke.

"Girl, this pussy is every bit as good as I knew it would be. Come on, I want to get you on the kitchen counter," he said, while peeling my gown off of me and the clothes off of him. "Come here and suck this dick before I get you over there."

I asked no questions nor uttered any words, but obediently obliged. He played with my throbbing nipples while I sucked away. Then he changed the plan. He laid my head on the arm of the sofa while spreading my legs. As he placed his big dick back inside my mouth, he inserted his tongue in my pussy along with his finger in my ass. I tried to suck the black off his dick. It took no time for me to cum, as it didn't take him long to relieve himself deep inside my throat. I typically have a rule against a man cumming in my mouth, but it seemed all rules had gone out the window.

Just when I thought he was spent, Lewis carried me to my bed and began licking and sucking my lovely double-D's that turn all heads. Oh, it felt so good. He used a free hand to massage my pussy right before placing his ten inches inside. That time, it felt more like we were making love. He was so tender and passionate. I pretended he was my husband.

I completely lost track of time. Looking at the clock, I saw it was nine o'clock. *Oh my goodness, I'm late for work!* Lewis lay spent, still inside and on top of me. I was feeling so damn good that I didn't want him to move. I could still feel his dick pulsating inside of my pussy.

Finally, I spoke up. "Lewis, I have to call my job. You have to get up."

"We're not done yet, so don't tell them you'll be in before noon," he answered.

That sounded intriguing to me. I hurried and called my job, telling them I had a doctor's appointment I forgot about and would be in as soon as I was done. Since I normally have perfect attendance, they didn't push the issue.

"Come here and suck my dick again," Lewis said after I hung up the phone. "It's going into that asshole next. I've been thinking about getting my dick up in that fat ass ever since the first time I slid my fingers up in there."

"Huh?" was all I could manage to get out before his dick was back in my mouth again. This time, it seemed less pleasant. He was talking to me like some street whore. I tried to rationalize it as him role playing to help me get with the program. Then he started pulling my hair and pushing his dick in deeper. At this point, I don't know what to think.

He abruptly stopped and laid me on the bed facedown with my legs hanging off the bed. He started licking my asshole and fingering my pussy. Then he pulled the fingers out, positioned himself, and slid his dick inside my pussy. He stroked harder than he did previously, but it felt good. His testicles were slapping my ass on one side while his hand slapped the other side, causing a stinging sensation that shot through me. He was back to the hair pulling again. Then the stroking stopped, and the penetration in my ass came. He wasn't too gentle about it, but he worked it all the way in. He reached one hand around the front of me to fondle my clit and the other hand fondled my breast. Oh, it hurt so good.

The multi-positioned sex went on until around 11:30 a.m. He then went and took a shower, calling me in there as well to suck him some more while he returned the favor. He fucked me one last time in the shower before getting out and getting dressed. Me? I was on cloud nine.

He started towards the door, but then stopped and turned to me. I thought he was about to kiss me because he placed his hands on both sides of my face.

"You know, Charise, I thought about this pussy for the longest. I have fucked my wife many nights, pretending she was you. I masturbated to the thoughts of when I fingered and licked you at my other place. I imagined your tits in my mouth when I sucked Sandy's tits."

At this point, he had my ego grinning from ear to ear.

Then he continued. "But, no matter how much pussy you give me, you will never be half the woman your sister is."

I quickly pushed away from him. I didn't see that one coming.

He went on to say, "See, you're a trifling bitch—the lowest form of trifling. You have no problem fucking your sister's man. You would put a piece of dick before your own blood. That's low! But, I ain't gonna lie. Your pussy was everything I hoped for and then some, and I'd love the chance to do it again when the opportunity permits."

I was astounded, crushed.

"You have the nerve to say all that hurtful shit to me, and then want to do it again? Are you psycho?!" I yelled.

He arrogantly chuckled while walking towards me. "No, baby, I'm just stating the facts. Your trifling ass actually turns me on. It's not like you can tell anyone about this experience. Sandy will be in town later today and didn't think it was a problem with my being here while you were at work. She's flying back the day after tomorrow. My flight is scheduled to leave on Saturday, as well. However, I would like to get some more of your pussy before I go back to Denver," he stated matter-of-factly.

I stepped away from him, bumping into my sofa—the same sofa we had just finished making love on moments before.

"Lewis, you need to get out of my damn apartment, now!" I yelled.

He walked towards me and put his arms around me like he never said a word. By this time, I had tears in my eyes. He held me tight, as if he were my man trying to comfort me from someone else. When I tried to push him away, that's when he decided he wanted to kiss me. I continued trying to push him away from me, but he held me with one arm and used his other hand to fondle my clit as he was bending to kiss my lips. With his fingers now inside my pussy, he continued kissing me.

Damn, I'm pissed off with him, but it feels good as I don't know what.

The resistance my mouth was screaming was definitely out of sync with my wet pussy and throbbing tits.

Ain't this a bitch? He already thinks I'm stupid for fucking him. Oh well, the damage is already done, I thought to myself.

So, there we were once again fucking in my living room, on the other chair this time. We eventually found our way to the kitchen counter.

You know what? Fuck Sandy! I'm going to enjoy this dick every chance I get. I guess he said it right: I'm trifling and less of a woman than Sandy. But, whose pussy does he want more than Sandy's? Mine! And he'll have it whenever he wants it. Anytime.

4
Kelly

Thankfully, I'm nothing like my sisters. At twenty-six, I know how to enjoy my life without compromise. I like meeting people and having options. However, when it comes to men, I have my three-month rule. Most guys don't make it past two weeks. Charise thinks that's about the time I give in and then get kicked to the curb. WRONG!

I like fine dining and receiving nice gifts. I make it clear from day one about my three-month rule. Unfortunately, some guys think after a nice dinner and some flowers or stuffed animals, I'm supposed to just lose my damn mind and give up the goods. Not Kelly Marie Wiggins. Those who successfully got some spent plenty before getting it. And if they don't hang around after that, then I'm like, "Oh well. Next!"

I wouldn't consider myself materialistic or a prostitute, but I feel it is a tragedy for women to let men use their bodies and not have anything to show for it. I like sex just as much as the next one; however, I have more respect for my body than the next one. I also think it's a tragedy to have given up the goods and feel like a man has taken advantage of you. You don't get to know everything about a man in three months, but you certainly know more than you would have in less than three months. Most will show their true colors within six months.

Also, for the ones that make it to three months, I run a credit and background check on them. The ones who get the axe as a result of that check get angry about it. They would have all kinds of domestic violence, DUI's, and child support issues, not to mention raggedy credit, but won't dare volunteer such information. They get angry that I would wait three months to run this check because they would have spent their monies for three months and never received my goodies. One might think I'm wrong for letting them spend their money for three months, but those are the ones who didn't know I make it a point to inform guys during our very first date of this practice. I guess they thought they would just woo me to the point that I would lose my mind and drop my drawls. And once you give it up, you can't get your pussy back. He had you, and at the very least, you better get yours. When it comes to my body and self-respect, there is no compromise. I would hate to shame my now deceased momma, who always made it a point to tell me how proud she was of my uncompromising personality.

Another fallacy my sisters have is they believe I pick up my dates from nightclubs just because they see me flirting. The truth is, in eight years of dating, I have only dated two guys I met in a nightclub. That was at least three or four years ago. Those two made it bad for all to follow. When I go to the clubs, I like to have fun, but I leave it right there.

I started my own event planning company after graduating college. So far, so good. Being in the D.C. Metro area, I tend to yield some well-to-do clients. I have to admit, as much as I can't stand Elaine, she is always throwing business in my direction. Most of these people shop in her shoe store. There has been times when I had so much business I didn't know what to do. My dear reliable sister, Harmony, would always be the first to my rescue. She'd round up extra staff for me, jump in and work herself, or simply function as a mental outlet when

I'd get overwhelmed. I talk a lot of crap about Harmony, but she's actually my hero.

I also make it a point of having all my dates meet Harmony. She has an outstanding ability to pick up on idiosyncrasies I may have not caught on to. I wouldn't let them know she's a psychologist ahead of time. I often feel sorry for Harmony because between her profession and six siblings, who she is always available for, she doesn't have a social life beyond our girls' night out. No male prospects are knocking at her door, although she says she's okay with it. I do call her at least once a week to let her know how much I love and appreciate her.

"Hey, Elaine," I answered, seeing her number on my caller ID. *Hopefully, she's calling with a new client.*

I hated when she called while I was trying to watch my *Young and the Restless* at night on the Soap Channel.

"Hey, little sister," Elaine responded. "Did I catch you at a bad time?"

"I'm just working on a contract," I lied. "Why, what's up?"

I didn't dare let Elaine know I was doing something meaningless like watching soap operas. Otherwise, she would start threatening not to send me clients because my priorities were all screwed up. My plan was to take a hot shower after my show went off, stimulate myself until I had an explosive orgasm, go to bed, and get up the next morning all refreshed to work on those contracts for real.

"Girl, we're going back to Megaplex on Wednesday, right?" she asked, shocking me to no end.

"Elaine, you want to go back to Megaplex? What happened to you trying to be supportive of Russell? I was hoping to switch things up," I told her.

"Oh, fuck Russell! I had a good time at Megaplex, and I promise I'll even leave Renee home this time," she pleaded.

"I know about you and Mandingo."

Elaine gasped so hard she almost choked. Then she stuttered, "But, but how? How could you know about Mandingo?"

I responded, "Remember, I saw you in the club. I saw how you had your tit in his mouth."

I heard Elaine give a sigh of relief. "Oh, girl, I forgot all about that."

"I bet you did, liar! You sounded kind of nervous there for a minute, like you might be hiding something," I laughed. "However, I hate to disappoint you, but the exotic dancers were a one-shot deal. They are not at the Megaplex on a weekly basis."

"Well, where are they going to be next week?" she probed.

Now I really knew something was up. "Okay, what's really going on here?" I asked. "I hope you're not trying to hook up with Mandingo."

"Why would I do something like that, Kelly? I simply found it entertaining," she lied.

"Well, I hope that's all there is to it, because Mandingo sure had his face under Shawnee's skirt before he was over there sucking on your tits. Oh, but you missed that part, sitting over there on the other side," I told her.

"Oh really?" Her tone suddenly switched to pissed off. "And you saw this with your own eyes?"

I found it amusing how her attitude suddenly changed with that bit of info. So, I answered, "Saw it with my own eyes."

"But, Shawnee has a husband. Why would she let him do that to her knowing she's married?" Elaine demanded to know.

"Calm down, Elaine! It's not like his big ass took the time to ask questions. She was trying to push him away, but he took over," I replied. "So now I know you got busy with Mandingo."

"How would you make that leap?" she tried to say in a firm voice, but the higher pitch was a dead giveaway.

"Ooh, Elaine! You slept with Mandingo!" I announced.

"I don't know what you're talking about. I have to go now," she lied.

This was better than *The Young and the Restless*.

"Go ahead and hang up, 'cause I need to call the Wiggins girls and share this tidbit of info," I threatened playfully.

She choked and stuttered, "Kelly, I will kill you! You better not say a word."

I laughed so hard. Miss Attitude was busted, which would provide me leverage on a later date when she tries to talk down to me.

"Details," I insisted.

"Kelly, don't make me do that," she pleaded.

"Elaine, it's obvious that you're dying to tell someone, so spill it. You know I have never violated your confidence," I lied, knowing I shared her dirt every chance I could get.

"Okay, okay!" she squealed. "Girl, while he was working me over in the club, he passed his phone number to me. I called him and hooked up that next night. He cooked me a nice lobster dinner that took a few hours before we got to eat."

"Why is that?" I asked.

"Why do you think?" she responded.

"Hours?" I asked.

She repeated, "Hours! He didn't leave anything undone. So, after dinner, we had an encore session. I think the sun was coming up by the time I got home. And his size gave him every right to call himself Mandingo."

"Wow!" was all I could say. "Are you planning on seeing him again? He doesn't seem like the ideal boyfriend material, particularly after what I saw him doing to Shawnee."

Elaine sighed. "Augghh! Please don't remind me. I wasn't looking to make him a boyfriend. I just like the way he do what he do."

"What about Russell? How are you going to juggle it all?" I asked out of genuine concern.

"I don't know. I think you're right. I need to chalk it up to a one-time experience. I could have easily called him, but I didn't want to come off as some bitch jocking him. I figured if I see him in the club, then we could just hook up from there," she explained.

"Elaine, the problem with that is I don't think you would feel too great if you went back into a club and witnessed him with his next prey. There's no telling how many women at the Megaplex last Wednesday were there with the same intentions," I advised. "And Lord knows how many women he passed his number to. For all we know, he could have passed it to Shawnee, also. If he was licking all between her legs, I don't see why he wouldn't have given her his number."

"Uh-uh! Licking between her legs?" Elaine sounded even more pissed off.

"I said his head was underneath her skirt. Hell, his hands were under yours, and from what I saw in your face, he found what he was searching for," I laughed.

"Shut up! You better not say shit about that to anyone."

"Who am I going to tell?" I lied, knowing full well I had already told. "Don't nobody give a shit. We were just out having a good time, and you got yours. I just don't want you playing yourself like all those other women who were out there hoping for another go round with him."

"Damn, you're my little sister; I'm supposed to be giving you advice. Thank you, Kelly," a humble Elaine said, then added, "And to show how much I appreciate your words of wisdom, I'm not going to put up any resistance to whatever you decide for us on Wednesday."

"Are you getting a sensitive side in your old age?" I laughed.

"Who are you calling old, winch?" She laughed. "Take note that I only said Wednesday, not from now on. And I mean it, Kelly; you better not say a word about what I told you or what you saw."

"Scout's honor," I lied.

"You ain't never been in any damn scouts, trick."

We laughed together, and then I shifted gears.

"I didn't tell you the real reason Sandy came to town this past weekend, did I?" I asked Elaine.

"She came following behind that jackass Lewis, who had some child support issues to handle. I guess she didn't trust him in his old stomping grounds," she answered.

"WRONG!" I announced. "That was her excuse to come."

"Spill it, Kelly. What do you know?" Elaine asked.

I informed her, "She came to hook up with her ex-boyfriend Eric."

"Eric?" she asked.

"Yeah, I'm not sure if you remember her talking about some guy Eric a while back. She used to brag about him being so big," I added.

"I think I do remember. Why would she want to come visit her ex-boyfriend, when she spends all of her energy chasing Lewis?"

Elaine's tone began to give rise to anger, and I picked up on the attitude change.

"I don't know, Elaine. Maybe she's tired of playing the fool. You sound angry, though."

Elaine tried to calm her tone. "I just get pissed off when it comes to her stupidity behind Lewis. So, instead, she goes and screws an ex to try leveling the playing field. It's retarded."

"You are so right. It is annoying as hell. I wonder who Lewis was doing while she was busy doing Eric," I commented.

"Probably one of his baby's mommas," she laughed. "Girl, we are sitting on this phone like neither one of us have things to do," she added.

"Yeah, I have to get back to my contract," I lied still. "You have me on this phone gossiping."

"I know your ass is probably watching those damn soap operas. Lying ass talking about some damn contracts at nine-thirty at night."

We both laughed.

After we hung up, I pondered on Elaine's reaction when I told her about Sandy hooking up with her ex. I didn't have to be a rocket scientist to figure out something was wrong with that reaction.

Since Harmony is the psychologist, maybe I'll just run it by her.

5

Harmony

Sometimes I hate having a bunch of sisters. They keep so much mess. When I speak with other women who also have many sisters, they seem to echo my sentiments. However, I can't imagine there being another set as nutty as mine. I should do like Sandy and pack up and move away. With everyone having free domestic calling plans on their phones these days, that would mean I'd have to move out of the country to get some peace.

All of them treat me like their personal psychologist, to the point where I need therapy. I continually try to convince them to hook up with their own therapist, but they don't see the logic since they have me. They say they don't like strangers all up in their business, but then their lifestyles alone keep everyone in their business. Charise shows any man "her business" just for a drink or a few kind words. Sandy is so damn loud that you can't help but hear her business. Kelly is Miss Social Butterfly and has a mouth that runs like a broken faucet. Shawnee doesn't know the meaning of discretion when it comes to her using her sexuality to get what she wants professionally. Now Elaine, that's a tight-lipped one there. Still, she needs help learning how to stop talking down on people. At least she doesn't bother me like the others, though. Yeah, she's the sneaky ass. Always up to something, but she keeps her mouth shut about her business, except to Kelly who tells it all.

I can't wait for my own therapy appointment on Thursday. I have to go just to be able to deal with my own family. Most psychologists go to therapy to keep from getting overwhelmed by their work. I go to keep from getting overwhelmed by my family. Then the bitches want to tie up my time with their drama, pick my brain, and don't feel I have the right to tell them that they should be paying for my professional services. They really believe I don't have any feelings. Since I'm not the argumentative type, they confuse that with my lacking a backbone. I bet if I started spilling all of their dirt, they'd find some respect for me then.

Now, because of their trifling asses, I'm going to have to pay for an extra hour in therapy. I know my therapist is sick of them, as well. I usually go there to share the dirt of my siblings. Wait until I tell my therapist how my only brother decided to confide in me that he's a closet homosexual. I guess I can forget about nieces or nephews from Angelo. He's still not ready to share that info with the family. Even worse, he's the feminine one in his relationship. Hmm, you think having six sisters influenced his behavior? I don't know how we missed it as he was growing up. Probably because of our large age gaps and because Momma shielded Angelo as if he were the Messiah, which made none of us want to be around his spoiled ass. She made us get in the street to fight the neighborhood, but not her precious Angelo. She wasn't going to risk her baby being hurt.

In therapy, I also have to talk about my married sister's full-blown affair with my younger sister's ex-boyfriend. I thought she would have stopped it once I told her who Eric Bradshaw was, but she has hooked up with him every day since she met him last Wednesday. For the life of me, I can't figure out how he manages the time. From what Kelly has "confided" in me, Elaine told her that she's sleeping with Mandingo. Only Kelly doesn't know Mandingo and Eric are one and the same. However, Elaine is fully aware that Eric is Sandy's ex-boyfriend. My telling Shawnee about Sandy also didn't matter. So, to add a twist, Sandy shows up for an "old time's sake" romp in the hay with Eric.

In a nutshell, he slept with three of my sisters within a matter of days. I truly want to beat his ass for that. I even thought about calling some of Momma's rougher family in Detroit to handle his ass. He can't possibly look at my sisters and not see the spitting resemblance. They even have a similar build. Sandy is a bit heavier and less tight in the body, but still similar enough to see a resemblance.

Oh, but the icing on this week's cake came when Charise "needed someone to talk to." She was turned out by Lewis, then wanted to share all her erotic details with me. I almost threw up. I should have known it was bound to happen. I was just surprised it hadn't already happened. My sisters give "between sisters" a whole new meaning. No matter how ridiculous Kelly's three-month rule may seem, I have to give it to her. She doesn't allow herself to get caught up in the nonsense that the others do.

We've been doing the girls' night out since Momma's death, but I feel I am nearing my cutoff point. I just don't get excited at the thought of meeting up with them. Prior to Momma's illness, everyone was doing their own thing as if we lived in different parts of the world. We called each other every once in a blue moon out of pure obligation because Momma used to press us to be close to one another like she was with her own large family of ten (aka The Wyatt Clan). I probably talked to Sandy more than anyone because of her children that I always seemed to be babysitting somehow. Momma's illness brought Shawnee and Kelly closer in the fold. Shawnee and Sandy seemed to always have this underlying tension between them, but were more tolerant as sisters if anything. They'd always have each other's back if there was a problem from an outsider. That's probably a big part of the reason Shawnee's still screwing Eric despite his relationship with Sandy.

Tomorrow is another Wednesday, and they want to go back to Megaplex. At least this time is karaoke, so it shouldn't be too bad. I make it a point to go to therapy the day after our girls' night out. I always need that immediate release after putting up with their Wednesday night foolishness.

Dealing with the issues of six siblings leaves me no time for my own social life. My last relationship was four years ago. I was involved with a fellow psychologist who couldn't tolerate my family. He wanted me to choose between them and him. Obviously, I chose my family. I understood where he was coming from, but I lost respect for him for asking me to choose. It was even worse for him to ask it while my mother was sick battling cancer.

When I'm out with my sisters, there are many men who hit on me, but I don't see them as suitable mates. There have been times when my raging hormones have considered a "temporary relationship", but my sisters are a reality check for me, as well as their consuming my free time.

I haven't had a real vacation in ages. I made the mistake of going on vacation with my sisters shortly after Momma died. We ended up at some raunchy resort in Jamaica. I was feeling quite old compared to the endless college girls walking around naked and sexing anything that moved. Elaine opposed being there, and that was one time I wished she had her way. I think we would have ended up somewhere much classier. It would have probably been expensive as hell, but classier. Shawnee wasn't too thrilled either, until all the help at the resort were tripping over themselves to shower her with attention. Since that disastrous experience, I tell my sisters I can't take off time for a vacation each time they ask.

I do want to take a vacation on my own. Perhaps I'll go somewhere secluded with a nice spa. I'll have to keep this one under wraps so none of my sisters rearrange their schedules and volunteer to come along and keep me company. Yeah, I think I'll tell them when I return. Maybe I'll go on one of those 21-day excursions somewhere. Anywhere far away from them should be good.

Maybe I should start exploring some career moves away from D.C., as well. I have been here pretty much all of my thirty-five years of life. I think I'll go see a travel agent tomorrow. I'll give them a dose of how their lives will be when I do move away. Yep! That's what I'll do.

PART TWO

What's Done In The Dark...

6

Kelly

"Charise, how in the hell did you let something like this happen? Do you even know who the father is?" I asked.

Charise was sobbing uncontrollably at my table. "It just happened."

I gave her some tissue to clean herself up and attempted to give her a half-ass hug. I was so angry I could have strangled her.

Where the hell is Harmony when you need her? How could she just up and go on vacation, leaving me for Charise to announce her three-and-a-half month pregnancy. I'm not sure what to say to her. Harmony would know what to say.

"I'm going to call Shawnee over. I think she'd know what to do," I announced.

"Kelly, please no! Shawnee will never understand," Charise pleaded, jumping up from the chair to grab my arm as I reached for the phone.

"Hell, I can't understand," I told her. "I can't deal with this by myself. I don't know what the right thing to say is. I call Harmony with all my problems, and now I can't reach her."

Charise just cried harder. I didn't know what to do. I was about to shift into panic mode. Hell, I wanted to cry.

"I'm sorry, Charise. I'm going to have to call Shawnee. It's not like you're gonna be able to hide this much longer," I reasoned.

She sobbed harder, giving up her protest, and I called Shawnee to come to my house right away. I wouldn't give her any details other than it concerned Charise.

Twenty minutes later, my doorbell rang. Uh-oh, it was Elaine. When I opened the door, she pushed past me and started looking around.

"Elaine, what are you doing here?" I asked.

"Where's Charise? What's wrong with my sister?" she demanded to know, ignoring my question. "I called Sandy. She said she's calling for a flight and will be here as soon as she can."

"Sandy?" I questioned.

"Where is Charise?" she asked again.

"She's in the bathroom. Did Shawnee call you?" I asked.

She gave me the "stupid" look. It was obvious Shawnee must have called her.

Just then, Shawnee was coming through my door peeling off her sunglasses.

"Hey, Elaine, you beat me here. You talk to Sandy?" she asked while looking around and then said, "Where's Charise?"

Again, I answered, "She's in the bathroom. Sandy?" I asked again, thinking if this was important enough of a matter for Sandy to fly in for. Well, at least Sandy knew how to handle all that baby stuff and pregnancy.

"I want to know what's going on. What's so urgent, and why is she still in the bathroom?" Elaine asked, still ignoring my question about Sandy.

I played with my fingers the way I do when I get excessively nervous, then just blurted out, "Charise is three and a half months pregnant." I jumped out of the way like I was the soon-to-be dead baby's daddy.

"What did you just say?" Shawnee calmly asked, though I knew she heard clearly the first time.

"Pregnant?" Elaine asked dryly with hands on hips. "By who? I called Sandy for that shit?"

"I don't know. She never said," I answered.

"Charise!" Elaine yelled out. "Get your ass out here now!"

I felt kind of sorry for Charise. I knew she was having a difficult time, but it was about to get worse.

Shawnee chimed in, following Elaine to bang on my bathroom door. "Charise, there's no point in trying to hide. Come on out and face the music."

Charise slowly appeared from behind my bathroom door like a scared child.

"I want to know who's the daddy so I can go kick his ass," Elaine threatened, cracking the kinks out of her own neck. "How could you let this happen? You don't even have a boyfriend. Is this the product of your one-night stands?" she asked Charise, barely letting her make it out of the bathroom.

Charise began sobbing so hard, Shawnee moved around Elaine to give Charise a big hug. Then she told her, "Don't worry, sweetie. We are going to get through this. You have five sisters who are going to spoil this baby shamelessly. Elaine called Sandy, and she's trying to get here for you, too."

Charise sobbed harder as they slowly walked into my living room, still embraced.

"Charise, please tell me how this happened," Elaine said. "You know you are queen of one-night stands. How could you be so reckless by subjecting a baby to growing up with no father?"

Through excessive sobbing, I heard Charise reply, "I know who the father is." Then she sobbed harder.

"Okay, sweetie, tell us who the father is," Shawnee tried to say in the calmest voice.

Talk about the calm before the storm. Shawnee could be harsher than Elaine at times, especially with no Harmony to calm her down. Her niceness meant get the info, find the guy, and then beat him down as though Charise getting pregnant was all his doing.

Charise foolishly fell for the okie-doke. I thought I heard her mumble, "Lewis."

"Lewis? Sandy's Lewis?" Shawnee's calmness began to give rise to rage as she stepped away from Charise.

"Oh, I heard her say Lewis as clear as day," Elaine instigated. "I think she has lost her fucking mind. Oh yeah, you just wait until Sandy gets here and finds this shit out."

Charise ran back into the bathroom sobbing like a wounded beast, while I just sat there speechless and in shock. Sandy was going to get on an airplane and fly across the country to be here for a sister that betrayed her in the worse way…with her own husband. Somebody needed to stop her, quick-fast.

"Let me see if I got this right," Shawnee began. "My little sister, who insists on having whoring one-night stands, decides to not only sleep with my other sister's husband, but then doesn't feel the need to exercise the same precaution she does with her one-night stands," Shawnee stated in a question-like manner. Then she lost it and went to the bathroom door, banging on it like a lunatic. "Charise! Get your ass out here right now! Your dumb ass can't hide in there forever. Get the fuck out of that bathroom before I kick this door in!"

Suddenly, I found words when I heard her threaten my defenseless property. "Oh no, you won't!" I retorted. "You can kick her ass all day long, but you won't be messing up my house."

Both Elaine and Shawnee began yelling for Charise to come out. If I had taken the time to find out Lewis was the father, I would have thought twice about calling Shawnee. *They are not going to just go away, so Charise might as well come out and accept her beat down,* I thought.

As if reading my mind, Charise opened the door. She was no longer crying.

"Okay, bring it!" she said, suddenly finding some balls. Charise stood 5'3", looking like David, against a 5'10" Shawnee, who stood as Goliath.

"Did this bitch just say 'bring it' like I won't knock the shit out of her?" Shawnee asked in a higher pitched, unbelieving tone as she stepped in Charise's face.

"Calm down, Shawnee!" Elaine said, while placing her body between Charise and Shawnee. "I would love to kick her ass, as well, but there's a baby here. Lewis's baby."

That last comment caused Shawnee to reach around Elaine and slap Charise in the face.

I rushed to grab Charise before this turned into a knockdown, drag-out fight inside my house of all places.

They shouted back and forth for a while before Shawnee finally broke down in tears.

"What the fuck am I supposed to tell Sandy? Obviously I'm going to have to be the one to tell her," Shawnee said. "How long have you been involved with Lewis? I thought you said nothing ever happened?"

Charise collected herself and answered, "I wasn't involved with him. When they came in town a few months ago, he showed up at my door unexpectedly. Everything caught me off guard. I just got caught up in the moment. I've been kicking myself since then." Tears began rolling down her cheeks once again.

"Charise, why didn't you just go to an abortion clinic so we could sweep all of this under a rug, and Sandy would never have been the wiser?" I asked.

"I've been to the clinic twice and couldn't go through with it," she answered.

"Charise, you have placed all of us in an impossible situation. How are we supposed to coexist with Sandy now?" Shawnee asked.

"Sandy's gonna kick your ass the minute you drop that baby. You do know that, right?" Elaine asked Charise. "She might kick that baby out of your ass if she actually was able to catch a flight."

"It's not too late to go to the clinic," I contributed. "This time, we can all go with you and help you through it."

"I'll have to agree," Shawnee added. "We don't have to tell Sandy the baby belongs to Lewis. Otherwise, we'll never be able to have another family gathering ever again without there being a war. Not to mention your baby will never have a father. Lewis is not going to leave Sandy to be with you."

Charise foolishly responded, "Actually, he said he's going to leave her to be with me. He was also happy when I told him about the baby."

"Oh my God, Becky," Elaine said in her snooty blonde girl voice. "How dumb is this girl?" she theatrically asked. "You can't be serious, Charise. Please tell me you're joking."

"Lewis said he loves me and always has. He said he wants us to have this baby together," Charise said, all excited.

"Charise, he doesn't do shit for his other two children," Elaine replied. "Sandy probably pays his child support for them."

I was stupefied; I couldn't believe Charise could be so dumb.

"Charise, you need to abort this baby!" Shawnee demanded. "Otherwise, when we are forced to choose who we will invite to family gatherings, it won't be you."

Boy, wasn't that a blow below the belt. Unfortunately, Shawnee was right. We would have to eventually draw sides between Charise and Sandy. And since Charise made the decision to be a low-down trifling bitch, we were going to have to side with Sandy.

"I think all of this is just as much Sandy's fault. She insisted on keeping that dog-ass despite all of our warnings. She even knew Lewis had his sights set on Charise, which is why she tried moving away," Elaine contributed.

"I don't know why Charise would want to be with Sandy's leftovers," Shawnee commented.

Shawnee suddenly realized her own hypocritical behavior with Eric because Elaine and Shawnee's demeanor showed guilt.

Elaine quickly changed up, saying, "Well, maybe we're being too hard on Charise. But, that baby has to go in order to save this family."

"I agree, Charise," I added. "This family would never have peace again. Don't you want the birth of your children to be a joyous occasion? This would be anything but joyous. The Wiggins family will not go on record as being man-sharers."

Again, the look of guilt crept upon Elaine and Shawnee.

Shawnee walked to the door and said, "Well, you do what you must, but I have to go now. If you need me to go to the clinic with you, call me." She put on her Bvlgari sunglasses, raised a hand up in the air, and made her dramatic exit.

"I guess I better get going myself. I need to hurry up and stop Sandy from coming," Elaine said as she headed to the door. "Let me know what you decide." Then she was out the door.

I know what I just saw with Shawnee and Elaine, and I will get to the bottom of it. Right now, I have to get Charise out of here. I don't feel like being bothered with her stupidity.

"Okay, Charise, you're gonna have to get going. I have a lot of work to do, and I now have a headache from hell. Hell, I need a damn drink," I said, going to my bar to pour myself a shot of Henny.

"What am I supposed to do?" she asked.

I waved my hand while chugging the drink down my throat. "That's entirely up to you, Charise. It seems no matter what we say, or you knowing right from wrong, you're going to do what Charise wants to do," I responded, pouring another shot of Hennessey.

"Fine, I'll work out my own issues," she said as she stormed to the door. "I don't know why I wasted my time coming over here," she added, then was out the door.

"That doesn't sound too good," I said out loud to myself. "Where the hell is Harmony?!"

When I called Harmony last week, her voicemail said she was on vacation out of the country for a month. She didn't tell any of us that she was thinking of going away, and I wondered why. No one even knew where she went to.

Bitch! Hope the burglars call and find out she's gone.

7

Shawnee

Talk about the pot calling the kettle black. I have been sleeping with Eric on an almost daily basis since we met. Robert's lack of attention prevents him from catching on. In over three months, Robert and I had sex a total of five times. You can't tell me that he doesn't have something on the side, and with me having Mandingo, I don't give a shit.

I wouldn't leave my marriage to be with Eric. He's hardly somebody I'd want a commitment with, but the sex is to die for. I guess I can understand Charise to an extent when it comes to the dick making you throw all caution to the wind. At least Eric is an ex and not someone's husband, and at least I'm not trying to have his baby. Nonetheless, I realize I'm going to have to end things with Eric. It won't be easy, but I'm going to have to do it. I'll tell him after our date tonight. He's doing a show out of the country for the next few days. Hopefully that will make this break up easier.

I know Charise is not going to listen to a word we said. How can I blame her? I haven't listened to a word Harmony has said to me about Eric. At least if I put an end to this now, Sandy never has to know.

As usual, the sex was wonderful. Eric prepared a great lamb dish.

This man had some serious skills. He aspires to open his own upscale restaurant someday soon. He said his dancing will help fund his restaurant. He even had a business plan put together already.

This night, he privately danced for me to a Keith Sweat medley with a cow-hide cloth girded around his pelvic area. His large chest was covered in flavored oil, and his lengthy dick grew as he gyrated closer to my face while I sat in the assigned chair he placed me in for these private dances. He stepped back, took one of my feet, and rubbed it underneath his cloth, making contact with his large, exposed testicles. He grinded slowly up my leg until he was straddled over me and his big dick sat in my lap.

Each time I tried to touch his body, he'd restrain my hands. He undid the buttons on my blouse with his tongue. It was driving me crazy. I wanted him to suck the milk glands from my titties, but he wouldn't. He just continued to tease me, rubbing his g-string covered penis in my face and pulling back if I licked out my tongue.

He stood me up and removed the skirt I had worn from the office, sitting me back down with only my thong on. Again, he lifted my foot, this time taking one toe at a time into his mouth. My pussy was going crazy just from the sucking. My nipples were hard and begging for his mouth, but he made them wait. I attempted to rub my own pussy and tits, but again, he moved my hands. He had me feeling so good and frustrated that I wanted to cry.

Finally, his mouth left my foot and slowly made its way up my leg. When his face made it to my thighs, I parted my legs to allow access to the wetness that waited. He kissed the insides of both thighs softly until he reached my pelvis. By this point, I was already moaning loudly. He parted my thighs and his long tongue licked my pussy in one long stroke, bottom up. His tongue crept its way up to my navel as my whole body quivered. His large hands savagely took hold of my breasts while his tongue slid between them.

Keith was crooning from the speakers, and I heard something about "I'll do you…" I was feeling every single word. I heard him saying something about licking me from head to toe, and thankfully, my imagination didn't have to stretch too far, as Eric did just that. Keith was begging in the song, and my nipples were begging to be sucked in a way that only Eric could do.

When I couldn't take the teasing anymore, I whispered, "Please, baby, suck these titties. Suck them! Please!"

Eric looked intensely into my eyes just before his mouth attempted to swallow one of my large breasts. Then he let his tongue focus on my nipple before repeating on the other breast. I cuddled his head for dear life. This made my pussy scream. I don't know what it is about my tits that make my pussy go crazy, but I was trying to position myself in the uncomfortable chair to make my pussy grind up against his chest while he was still sucking on my breast. He so graciously loaned my pussy his fingers to rub on as he continued on my tits. When my teeth started to sink into Eric's head, it was his cue to make his way back downtown and clean up the spill he had caused on "Aisle 9". And there was plenty of juice for him to clean up.

With Eric, things would never be that simple. He would never be classified as boring. He stood me up, bending me all the way over the chair, with my ass facing upwards and my legs pointing downwards. He parted my ass cheeks and rubbed in between my legs before moving my wet thong to bury his face in. His tongue stroked my clit, slid deep inside of my pussy, and then into my asshole. When the chair became unstable to hold me, he lifted my body, moved me to his bench-styled table, and laid me on my back before going back down to finish his exploration.

After he sucked me dry, and multiple orgasms later, he took me back to my spectator's chair so he could continue his erotic dance to Joe's "All The Things (Your Man Won't Do)." This time, he finally let go of his girded cloth and let me touch his body. As always, I became amazed watching his twelve inches of dick grow another two inches while taking it into my mouth. This night, that chair got the workout of a lifetime. Eric fucked me in about five positions just using that one chair, including upside down. He doesn't know the meaning of a quickie. For him, the five positions on the chair were considered his foreplay. Me, personally, I was good. I could have smoked a cigarette at that point (although I don't smoke), but since a good dick is so hard to find, I indulged Eric in every way to maximize the experience.

He stood me up and we danced together slowly, not leaving any gaps between our sweaty bodies. He winded his hips down until his tongue once again found my clit. He teased and tickled until my knees buckled, causing my body to slump forward. He wouldn't let me fall as his tongue worked its way back up my body, creating circles on my nipples and then nuzzling my neck.

Then he coaxed my body to return the favor. I let my tongue slide down his chest, tasting a mixture of strawberry-flavored oil and our combined salty sweat. When I was down and positioned, I buried my face to give him what he loved the most: sucking his balls. I licked, teased, sucked, and had him pulling my hair trying to stop me, but I wouldn't let up. I let my fingers trace his asshole before bringing them back to grip his massive dick that was doing its own dance. When Eric could stand no more, his strong hands pulled me up, and he kissed me as if his lungs were depending on the air from my lungs.

He picked me up and carried me to his sofa where he ate my pussy some more. He'd stop on occasion to ask me in his sensuously, deep voice, "You want me to stop? You had enough? You know I'm not going to stop until you tell me to."

I was in too much ecstasy to speak coherently, but he got his answer when my thighs tried to squeeze the brain out of his head. He pulled my legs apart and would not stop, but went in deeper.

When my body tried to run, he kept his grip on my legs, laughing and saying, "Where you think you're going? You didn't tell me you had enough."

I could only scream as his long, thick tongue went back deep into my pussy in search of my G-spot, and I grinded my pelvis against his face to assist him with his exploration and my explosion.

Unfortunately, all good things must come to an end, and tonight, this had to be ours. After our wild sex session, I tried to gather my nerves to have the inevitable talk, as we lay in his large bed cuddled the way I should have been with my own husband.

"Hey, baby, what's on your mind? You seem like something is bothering you," Eric asked, sensing something was wrong.

"Eric, I don't know any easy way to say this," I responded.

He looked genuinely concerned. "Just say what's on your mind."

I took a deep breath. "I'm going to have to make this our last night together. Not because of anything you have done. You have been absolutely wonderful."

"So what's the problem then?" he asked.

"I recently learned that you were involved with my sister, and I have been trying to block it out, but am not able to," I answered.

He looked down, then back into my eyes. "Shawnee, I have fallen in love with you. I have no intentions of being with Elaine anymore. I planned on telling her the next time she tried to call me."

I almost choked and fell off of the bed while backing away from him. *Did he just say Elaine? This man just said Elaine! Not Sandy, but Elaine.*

"Elaine!" I screamed. "You mean to tell me that you've been fucking Elaine?"

"Didn't you just say your sister?" he asked. He looked confused, as though his sleeping with Elaine and me were okay.

"Eric, I was referring to Sandy. Sandy is my sister, and so is Elaine, who I knew nothing about!" I yelled as I got up from the bed and searched for something to cover my nudity. "And then to make matters worse, you knew about Elaine being my sister and didn't give a damn. Oh, and wait! Did I just hear you tell me you love me?"

"Baby, calm down," he pled, also getting up from the bed.

"Don't tell me to calm down, you pig," I retorted.

"Look, Shawnee, when we started this, you knew what I was about. Over the months, we've spent a lot of time together and gotten close. I've been with you more than I have ever been with one woman since I started dancing. You accepted me with all my dirt and never passed judgment. When I started with Elaine, I didn't set out to be with your sister. I noticed a similarity in appearance and asked her if I already knew her. She said no. Eventually, I picked up on where I knew her from. She looks like you. I debated on how to handle the situation. I didn't want to tell her about you because I wasn't sure what kind of mess that was going to cause you," he explained. "I never linked you to Sandy at all, though."

"So you had to keep fucking her to keep the peace between us?" I asked, searching around his loft for my scattered clothes that were in multiple places.

"I told you, I already decided to cut her off if she calls again. Shawnee, I love you. You're the only woman I want to be with," he said as sincerely as he could. "I know you're a few years older than I am, but that doesn't even matter because we mesh. We work well together."

"Eric, I can't keep seeing you. This is the end of the road for us. I can't do this anymore," I told him.

"Shawnee, please don't do this to us," he pleaded, taking the clothes from my hands. "I'm not going to just let you walk out on us. I love you, Shawnee. Please hear what I'm saying."

"Just like I knew what you were when we started, you knew I was a married woman," I spat, snatching my clothes back from him.

He laughed. "You were an unhappily married woman. The only reason you're happy now is because of what we share. I know that man doesn't love you like I can. Shawnee, I know you have to feel something for me. I know what we have is real."

"Stop it, Eric! What do you expect, for me to leave my husband? Do you suppose I keep being adulterous forever?" I asked as my disloyal nipples stood up once again, begging me not to leave. I tried hard not to look at his non-erect dick that dangled at least eleven inches.

"Baby, I don't know what I expect. I just know where I am right now." He walked to me, took my clothes yet again, dropped them to the floor, and touched my nipples with the back of his index fingers. He wrapped his large arms around me tightly before kissing me tenderly.

Somehow, we made love at that moment. It never quite felt like that before, but it was wonderful.

This will be the last time.

8

Elaine

"Hey, baby. Did I catch you at a bad time?" I asked when Mandingo answered the phone. *Time for my weekly fix.*

"Ummm, well, not really," he responded dryly when catching on to my voice.

"Will you be available later tonight?" I asked.

He answered my question with his own. "I have to ask you a question. Is that alright?"

I didn't hear any usual seduction in his voice, and he evaded my question. Not good.

"What's up?" I asked hesitantly. "You don't sound too happy to hear from me."

"When were you planning on letting me know you're Sandy's sister? You seemed to leave that bit of info out when I first asked where I knew you from," he responded, annoyed.

"Mandingo, this is just a sex thing. I didn't feel it was necessary to disclose that," I replied.

"So do you make it a habit of going around doing your sister's men?" he asked.

Now I was getting annoyed. *How is this whoring motherfucker questioning what I do?*

"You know, I really resent your accusation."

"Ever since Sandy left here a couple of months ago, I have been trying to put it together…" he started before I cut him off.

"Let me get this right. You slept with Sandy a couple of months ago?" I asked as if I didn't already know, then added, "Well, actually, it was over three months ago when she was in town."

"Me and Sandy will always have a connection. Just because she married a knucklehead doesn't mean a thing," he responded.

All I could say was, "Alrighty! You and Sandy?"

He answered, "You say that like you didn't know, when actually you knew the whole time."

"Hell, nigga, I was trying to do your sorry ass a favor. Shit, I thought you and Sandy were done years ago. I didn't know you currently had something going on with my sister," I told him. "Funny, your ass kept coming back for more of this knowing your self-righteous ass was still fucking her."

"Doing me a favor?" he rudely laughed. "Well, since I'm not done with your sister, I won't be getting with you anymore. Hopefully, I'll be able to survive without 'your favor.' So, this will most certainly be our last conversation."

"Wait! Wait a minute, Eric. This is getting way out of hand."

"You're the one talking about doing my sorry, self-righteous ass a favor," he chuckled.

"I know. I'm sorry. I take it back. We don't have to go out like this." My throbbing pussy started trying to reason. "Eric, who's going to know? It's not like anyone's going to find out. Sandy is way in Denver with her husband. I know you've been thoroughly enjoying this pussy and ass, not to mention the way I suck that big dick until you cum. It doesn't have to end here, you know?" I put it out there, hating to give up his lovely dick at the risk of playing myself.

He was silent for a moment, as though he was giving my proposition some thought.

"Elaine, you might be okay with it, but I certainly am not. So, give it up. We're done!" he sharply stated.

See, this is why you have to treat niggers like a trick. I get paid for my pussy, and the dumb ass that I gave some to for free wants to act like an ass.

"You know what? No problem, Mandingo. You won't hear from me anymore," I said, then hung up my phone.

I don't know what to say about this. Shit! Shit! Shit! Now I have to be nice to Russell's ass again. Hell, five tricks combined can't equal one Mandingo. Damn Sandy! Sneaking her ass over here to fuck Mandingo instead of the jackass she married. I guess that's why Lewis had plenty of time to impregnate Charise.

Who can I tell this shit to? Where is Harmony when you need her? No, I can't have Harmony in my business. Renee? No, she already tries to get all the dirt on my sisters and has no problem talking shit to them with whatever she knows. Besides, I don't want her to know I've been blowing Russell off for Mandingo. Never let a bitch have too much ammunition on you. Kelly! I can call Kelly. She already knows I slept with Mandingo.

9
Sandy

"Sandy, where you at? What's taking you so long? Come on in here before this water gets cold. Hell, you say I never do anything romantic, and now you got me waiting in this damn tub shriveling up like a raisin. Prune. I meant to say prune. Big Daddy's too big to shrivel up to a raisin. Bring that big ass on in here and warm Daddy up now."

What am I going to do? I am starting to show, and I can't continue to hide my pregnancy from Lewis. How do I tell him I'm pregnant but don't know if he's the father? I'm fourteen weeks pregnant. That is right about the time I slept with Eric. What was I thinking not taking some precaution? Hell, I've always been careful not to get pregnant by Lewis, but lost my damn mind when it came to Eric.

Lewis is going to be pissed off. Then again, I know that bastard slept with Charise. He thinks I'm so stupid. They both do. I called her job that day, and she missed work for the first time ever. I couldn't reach him or her by cell phone that whole day. Ironically, both of them didn't bother returning my call until eight o'clock that night. They called about five minutes apart and made up some bullshit story when I questioned what they did with their day. Charise told me she had company, but when I asked for details about the guy, she developed a stuttering condition along with being hard of hearing. Lewis can lie well, but he also did the stuttering thing.

My dumb ass was feeling fair is fair, and ran to the comforts of my reliable old flame, Eric. I didn't even see Lewis the whole time we were in D.C. I also noticed that every time I tried reaching Charise unsuccessfully, I was unsuccessful in reaching Lewis. Foolishly, I asked Lewis if he cheated on me while we were in D.C., and of course, he denied it. He claims he spent all of his time with his children.

I don't know why I thought moving Lewis to Denver was going to curb his whoring ways. Denver lacks black women, but has many white women who relentlessly seek black dick. I know with every fiber of my being that Lewis has screwed at least one of those white women. Then the few black women also shamelessly try to get my husband. It's like a fulltime job trying to keep tabs on him. Hell, I always got my kids trying to keep their eyes on his sneaky ass. They tell me that I need to leave him. I'm ready to pack it up and head back to D.C. At least there I don't have to sit around like some damn fool.

I don't know what Lewis will do once I tell him I'm pregnant. Will he try to play daddy of the year, or will he do his normal disappearing act? Even worse, what if he tries to be daddy of the year and it's not his baby? How did I get myself in this mess? Why didn't I just give Lewis the boot? What am I going to do with four children? One hundred thousand dollars doesn't go too far these days. What if this is Eric's baby? How will he feel about it? I should have stayed with Eric in the first place. He has more going for himself than Lewis.

"Sandy, I'm not going to keep calling you. If I get out of this tub, don't let me hear you complaining to me again about what I don't do for your ass. That's what's wrong with y'all damn women. You want to complain about what you don't have, but when a nigga tries to give ya what you want, then y'all wanna act all stupid. You better come on if you coming," he bitched from inside the large tub he had been waiting in for the past twenty-five minutes.

I walked into the bathroom and looked at that man like he fell and bumped his damn head. "Oh no the fuck you didn't just compare me to other women! Since you want to compare shit, you do have a fucking raisin compared to some prunes I've really had. Now! How you like that shit? And for the record, getting in the bath with you, scrubbing your nasty-ass back, and cleaning the crust from your funky-fucking toes is hardly my idea of romantic. What's worse is your bullshit idea of making the bathtub a Jacuzzi by farting in the water. It's fucking disgusting, you scumbag motherfucker! Get a damn house with a real fucking Jacuzzi, ya cheap bastard! Motherfucker, you must not know who you fucking with!" I yelled for Lewis and half of Denver to hear, taking a page out of Wilhelmina Wyatt-Wiggins' book. No doubt whose daughter I am.

Lewis stood up in the tub, and somehow, his dick rising up turned me the hell on.

"Shut that stupid shit up and come suck my dick!" he said arrogantly.

I stared at his dick for a moment. "Whatever! But I know you better not try comparing me to some other bitches," I said much softer while stubbornly making my way over to a waiting Lewis, who stood like Mighty Man with his fists resting on his hips.

His dick was standing at its full ten inches before I could kneel down and take it in my mouth. I hadn't even taken my clothes off yet, and as good as I was sucking his dick, he didn't give a shit. Somehow, after it was all said and done, I ended up in the tub washing his nasty back, crusty toes, and was the recipient of his personal Jacuzzi.

This is an example of a typical day in our lives. He talks shit, I have to check him, and then we end up fucking.

That next day while at work, I figured it was about time to tell the family to expect another baby. I decided to call Shawnee.

"Shawnee Wiggins here," she answered on the first ring.

"Hey, sis, you busy?" I asked.

"Never too busy for you," she responded. "You sound stressed. Everything okay?"

"If you call being pregnant and not knowing who the father is okay, then I'm wonderful," I lied.

I could hear Shawnee choking. She put the phone down while she tried to recompose herself.

"Oh my God, Sandy," Shawnee managed to say when she got it together. "How? Who?"

I laughed at her reaction. I didn't expect it.

"Well, I got pregnant the old-fashioned way, and the potential daddies are Lewis and one of my old boyfriends, Eric.

I could hear the phone drop.

"Shawnee!" I called out. "Shawnee, are you alright?"

"I'm here," she finally responded. "This is just a bit much for me. God, I now know how Harmony must feel having to listen to all of our problems."

"Why, what else is going on?" I inquired.

"Hold on, Sandy. There's a knock at my door."

Shawnee put the phone down, but I could hear someone tell her that she had a flower delivery.

She picked the phone back up and said, "Sandy, I'm going to have to go now."

"I could hear you received some flowers. I see Robert is trying to romance you again. I'm so jealous," I told her.

"Yeah, yeah, Robert," she answered. "I have to go now. Kiss the kids for me."

She hung up before I could get another word in. Something was going on for sure. I still hadn't found out what happened that day with Charise. *Hell, I have my own problems to worry about.*

10

Shawnee

I have to go somewhere so I can scream. I'm about to lose my fucking mind. Eric is bordering on stalking now. He's calling me twenty to thirty times per day. He's sending flowers almost every day to my job, along with stuffed animals that say "I love you." His phone messages are erratic. One moment he's "Baby, call me. I love you." Then the next moment, he's "Why the fuck are you doing this shit to us? We're not done yet." I guess he missed the rules of Booty Call class: There ain't any damn love or feelings. We're just supposed to do what we do and then keep it moving.

Now this is a man who has plenty of women and has been fucking not one, but apparently two of my sisters. Obviously, Sandy is not one of his exes. She's a current, as well.

I am beyond furious. Let's see. Two of my sisters are possibly going to have a baby at the exact same time by possibly the same man. Or the alternative to that, my sister is having a baby by the man I have been fucking for almost four months, who has the nerve to be stalking me now that I ended things. *Oh, I've got something for his ass.*

I picked up my phone to call Eric.

"Damn, girl, you finally called me back," he answered.

"Listen up!" I demanded. "You better stop all these fucking calls. It's over! Accept it and leave me alone. I don't want your flowers, stuffed animals, your phone calls, or you anymore."

"Shawnee, you can't do this to us." He sounded as if he were crying. "We belong together."

I retorted angrily, "Oh yeah, I can see it now: us raising your child that happens to be my niece or nephew."

"How would our child be your niece or nephew?" he asked.

"Note, I didn't say OUR child. I said YOUR child! The baby YOU will have within the next five or six months will be my niece or nephew. So again, Eric, I say leave me the fuck alone."

I was so pissed, tears were in my eyes.

"Shawnee, I don't know what you're talking about. I didn't get Elaine pregnant. We were both protected," he answered.

"Well, I guess you better figure out which other sister of mine you have fucked within the past four months," I yelled, forgetting I was still in my office.

There was a long pause before he finally said, "Sandy? Sandy's having my baby?"

"Yeah, you dumb bastard!" I said before slamming down the phone. Hopefully, he wouldn't call back ever again.

OOH! Oh my gosh! Oh my gosh! Oh my fucking gosh! I just told Eric about Sandy's pregnancy, and she doesn't know for certain. What is she going to think if he calls her and asks her? She's going to know I told him.

My phone rang, and it was Eric. AGAIN.

"What Eric?" I asked.

"Shawnee, are you serious about Sandy having my baby?" he asked sadly.

"No, Eric," I retracted to save face. "I just wanted you to admit you slept with another of my sisters. Three of us within four months? That is absolutely unforgivable. So now you can lose my number," I said, hoping he'd actually not call me again.

"Fine. If that's how you want to play this, I won't call you again," he said before hanging up on me.

Now I didn't know whether to be happy or start worrying. I sure didn't like the sound of that.

11

Kelly

"You want a glass of wine?" I asked Elaine when she arrived at my house.

"A glass of wine is definitely needed. You might want to find something stronger with what I'm about to drop on you, though," she responded.

"Uh-oh! That doesn't sound too good," I laughed, trying to stay lighthearted.

I poured Elaine a glass of wine, and taking her warning to heart, I fixed myself Hennessy on the rocks. Then I took the bottle to the coffee table in the living room where we were sitting. Elaine looked at her glass and then at the bottle of Hennessy.

"Okay, bitch, you brought a whole bottle for yourself, but only a glass for me," she said before we laughed.

Upon returning with the bottle of wine for Elaine, I said, "I hope you have an overnight bag with you, sis. You know I'm not going to let you drink a bottle of wine and then drive."

"You'll probably put me out before I can finish the one glass, after the mess I'm about to share with you," she replied.

All I could do was raise an eyebrow. I gulped down my drink and poured another before she could say anything. I did not like the sound of her words already.

"Damn, Kelly!" Elaine laughed. "It ain't that serious."

I responded, "That ain't what I just heard."

"It's time for some confessions," she said.

"I'm listening," I replied.

Elaine took a deep breath and then a sip from her glass. "Okay, here we go," she started. "Remember a few months ago I told you I slept with Mandingo?"

"Yeah," I answered.

"Well, I never ended it the way I said I would. I've been sleeping with him on a regular. That is until he just gave me the boot," she shared.

"Is that what you have been worried about telling me?" I asked, confused.

She made a "poof" noise with her mouth. "Hardly. One thing I never told you was Mandingo's real name."

"Why do I give a hoot about his real name? I never dated him," I responded, taking a sip of my drink.

"His name is Eric, and that would be the same Eric that Sandy shot into town to hook up with," she confessed, looking down into her glass.

I choked. "You have got to be kidding me," I responded when I recomposed myself.

"Unfortunately, I'm not." She sipped her wine and continued. "Even worse, I met him a few years back when Sandy introduced me to him while she was dating him. Not that it makes it any better, but I didn't know they were still involved when I got involved with him. You know how Sandy always said she doesn't go backwards."

"Bullshit!" I yelled out. "I personally told you that Sandy came here and slept with him, but your freaky ass had to keep sleeping with him after that. I can't believe you, Elaine." I took another gulp from my glass before refilling it, now without ice.

"I guess I had that coming, and you're absolutely right," Elaine contended.

"But, on top of that, you didn't end it. You waited until he gave you the boot," I reminded.

"Ouch!" was all she could say.

"So that would explain the guilt I picked up on while we were all jumping on Charise. Funny, I noticed the same reaction from Shawnee. Does she know the man that had his face between her legs is Sandy's boy-toy, also?" I asked.

"As far as I know, Shawnee never met him before. We all knew Sandy was involved with an Eric, but I can't see how she'd make the connection," Elaine responded.

"Well, I guess none of it matters anymore as long as you promise that you are absolutely done. Shawnee doesn't need to be involved. It's not like she's sleeping with him. Thankfully, she's married," I reasoned.

"You know I'm done, and I agree, Shawnee doesn't need to be involved. Lord knows I don't need her having eternal dirt on me," Elaine said with her hand held up to seal her promise.

I burst out laughing. The alcohol was kicking in. We continued drinking and laughing until we passed out.

12

Harmony

Bitches! Bitches! Bitches! Every last one of those sisters of mine. I have been gone for four weeks, and they have collectively managed to tie up my home, work, and cell phone voicemails. All of my voicemail boxes are filled and won't take any more messages. I have two messages from work-related items and forty-eight messages from them.

I absolutely refused to check any voicemails or emails while I was away. I'm sure I would have had more voicemails, but the poor mailboxes ran out of space two weeks ago. Those were the last sets of messages, and they were on my work voicemail. They had the audacity to leave me a message on my work line informing me that my other voicemails were full. I haven't bothered to inform them that I've been home for the past two days. I've spent that much time checking both voicemails and emails.

So now, Charise and Sandy are pregnant, possibly by the same jackass. That or Sandy is pregnant by the same man that both of her sisters are screwing. Sounds like some nasty-ass soap opera, where everybody is sleeping with each other's men. I really laughed at the fact that these idiots left a whole therapy session recorded on my voicemails, sharing all their foolishness. Now what if I never made it back to hear these messages? Some government authority would have had the laugh of a lifetime listening to their mess. Silly bitches!

My vacation was wonderful. Well, actually, it wasn't all vacation, but anything away from my family is a vacation. My first week was spent in Hawaii. My second week was in the Mexican Riviera. The third week I spent in Houston. I went there for a new job that I'll begin in six weeks. I also used that week to check out some homes. My fourth week was spent in Cancun with Todd, the absolutely gorgeous 6'2" doctor I met while at a restaurant in Houston.

The Cancun thing was very spur of the moment. Todd had just started his vacation the day before we met. When I let him know I had time left before my anticipated return to work, he suggested going away somewhere together. He suggested somewhere in Europe, but I know I couldn't handle too much more jetlag. So, we ended up in Cancun since I just did the west end the week before. It was a free trip with a gorgeous man, so I didn't put up too much resistance. Todd covered every cost of our vacation, and he wasn't a cheap tightwad. Out of all the places I've been in my life, nothing will ever top my week in Cancun. I couldn't have thought to pray for a better experience. Everything was perfect.

Todd is forty-three years old with two sons, ages 21 and 23. He owns a thriving medical practice in Houston, as well as a very nice home on a good piece of land. He has a wonderful sense of humor, excellent fashion sense, and a diverse dining style, all of which I greatly appreciate. Oh, did I mention how smart he is and that he has a smile and body to die for? I can actually have an intelligent conversation with him, and he respects our differences of opinions.

I had the opportunity to meet his parents, two of his four sisters, and one of his three brothers when we returned to Houston. They were a pleasant diversion from my own family. It's funny because before meeting Todd, I hadn't had any thoughts of marriage. After meeting and spending time with him and his family, though, I could actually see myself with him. Perhaps I'm getting ahead of myself, but it's a nice thought. Todd certainly differed from my last boyfriend, who wanted me to choose between him and my family. Todd promotes family closeness. When I shared some of my family insanity, he laughed and let me know he'd be my sounding board when I needed to vent, but reminded me that I'm the glue that holds the Wiggins family together, no matter where I relocated to.

I have given my four-week notice at work. I figure I'll use the other two weeks for my relocation to Houston. I still have to take a couple trips down there before I can leave D.C. for good. Now I have to get my home on the market. That part I'm not looking forward to. Oh, but I can't wait to get far, far away from D.C. and all the drama that my sisters keep.

The coup de grâce will be when Sandy moves back to D.C. and learns her sister is carrying her husband's baby. I'm trying to get out of dodge before that happens. The irony of it all, according to their many messages, their due dates are only two days apart. Oh no, I almost forgot! Sandy's other potential baby's daddy has been shamelessly stalking Shawnee. Go figure. I need to write a book about them. It'll probably make it to the bestseller's list.

I still have two more days before I need to return to work. I think I'll use the time to get my affairs in order. I'm certainly not going to let any of my sisters know I'm back in town until after I return to work. Better yet, until I've had an opportunity to consult with my own therapist. I need all the help I can get with this mess. I'm scared to tell Todd any of this for fear of frightening him away.

13

Shawnee

"Kelly, what the fuck am I going to do about this lunatic?" I asked. "I have threatened to call the cops on him, and he won't quit."

"Shawnee, I still can't believe you got yourself in this mess. Why were you sleeping with him?" Kelly asked. Then she continued before letting me respond. "So let me get this right. You, Sandy, and Elaine have been simultaneously screwing the same man? Sandy may be having his baby, and he has the balls to be stalking you?" She put her hands up in disbelief. "Ooh, no, no, no, no! Charise and Sandy may be having a baby around the same time, possibly by the same man? This is some sick shit, Shawnee."

"Tell me about it." I was an emotional wreck, pacing back and forth in Kelly's living room before plopping down on her sofa.

"Okay now, watch the sofa. I paid too much for it," Kelly warned in all seriousness. "I think you need to come clean with Robert and take whatever legal action you must against Eric. At least if you tell Robert yourself, you won't have to worry about what will happen if he finds out," she reasoned.

"Boy, don't you make that sound real easy. Robert will flip if I tell him that," I responded.

"Shawnee, what do you think is going to happen WHEN, not IF, he finds out? Hell, at least if you bring it to him, you could make it as though it's his fault for neglecting you. What was that song by TLC, 'Creep'?" She started singing the song. "Just like they said, no attention goes to show, so you crept. That's his damn fault. He's probably creeping his damn self."

She didn't tell any lie there. I really wouldn't have been so vulnerable if Robert wasn't neglecting me.

"Hell, you might have a point there. I do feel like it's partly his fault. I know I have to do something about Eric. He needs to be stopped," I said.

"Hey, I have an idea. Why don't you set up a meeting with him, Elaine, and Sandy there, and all of you confront his trifling ass," Kelly suggested.

"Let's see, that would mean someone would have to let crazy-ass Sandy know that her two trifling sisters have been sleeping with her possible baby's daddy." I shook my head. "Nah, I don't think so. Not a good idea."

"Well then, I say tell Robert and go from there," she advised.

"The problem with that is, if Robert somehow miraculously forgives me and joins forces with me to legally get Eric out of our lives, Sandy will eventually find out it was me that had her baby's daddy locked up," I answered.

Kelly looked as though she was processing everything. "Yeah, you have a point there." She paused. "Well, you can always move out of the country. That way, you'll be far enough away from Sandy, Robert, and Eric." She looked like she could be serious.

"Are you serious, Kelly?" I asked.

"I'm just saying..." She hunched her shoulders.

"Gee thanks!" I said.

"Look, Shawnee, I really don't know what to tell you. There are no easy answers, and many people will be affected by your actions. Not just your actions, but Elaine and Charise's actions. Things may not have been so bad if you all weren't trying to keep the dicks between sisters. You could have had your affair with any other man except Sandy's, just like Charise."

"Boy, you know it's fucked up when you get classified with your baby sister," I stated. "Kelly, I fucked up, and now I need to sleep in the bed I made. And for the record, I had no idea about Elaine or Sandy when I first started with Eric. I eventually learned that he was Sandy's ex, and I should have stopped it there."

"My God! No wonder Harmony ran away from home without telling us. This mess is too much for poor me. I can just imagine having all your messes dumped on her daily," Kelly expressed.

"Wow, you made that sound as though you never drop your bunch of issues on her," I responded.

"My issues are nothing compared to all of your issues. Shoot, now we have to pick a sister to side with. Once all the shit hits the fan, no one will be speaking to anyone, anymore. Momma will be rolling over in her grave. And wait until Elaine finds out about you sleeping with Eric, too. She only knew about Sandy," Kelly warned.

"Elaine is not in a position to say shit to me. She knew all along about Eric and Sandy," I answered.

"I'm just saying." Kelly hunched her shoulders again. "Even Charise is going to be pissed after the way both you and Elaine jumped on her."

"A baby is a big difference! It's something that can't be swept under the rug. A baby is forever. The child will never have the opportunity to spend time with his or her aunt and cousins. Sandy wouldn't ever have anything to do with that child, even if her baby turns out to be Eric's baby."

"Yeah, no matter how you slice this, Sandy is going to be an unhappy person," Kelly stated. "Let me ask you a question."

"Go for it."

"Was the sex really all that to make the three of you just lose your ever-loving minds?" she chuckled. "That had to be one powerful dick, tongue, or whatever to just make you all not give a damn about the consequences.

"Ha ha! Very funny. But, to answer your question, it was definitely a once-in-a-lifetime experience."

"Damn, you're making me jealous. A once-in-a-lifetime experience?" she repeated. "Wow!"

14

Harmony

"I think you need to tell Eric about the baby," I suggested in an effort to get Eric to back off from further stalking Shawnee and her having to go public, hurting everyone.

I haven't been home a whole week and already trying to do damage control. My therapist made the suggestion, and I thought it might work.

"Harmony, I can't do that. What if the baby is not Eric's, but Lewis' instead?"

"I think Eric has the right to know. Just let him know it's only a possibility. You obviously want the baby to be his anyway. Isn't that why you're planning to return to D.C.?" I reasoned.

"What am I supposed to do about Lewis?" Sandy asked.

"What about him? You obviously didn't give a damn about Lewis while you were unprotected with Eric. Lewis has other children that he obviously didn't stand behind when he left to go to Denver. I don't see Lewis as someone giving a damn about anyone other than himself."

"That you're probably right about. So how would I do this? Over the phone or in person?" Sandy asked.

Yes! She's going for it.

"Sandy, I think the sooner the better. You're pretty far along already. Just call him now and tell him. Lewis hasn't been all too receptive when you told him you were expecting, right?"

"When I told Lewis, he hit the roof. He asked if I were trying to make the Brady Bunch. He couldn't understand why I didn't just go and get an abortion while it was early enough," Sandy answered.

"And you didn't leave his ass then?" I asked, more annoyed than the last time I heard the mere mention of Lewis' name. "Well then, it's settled. You make that call now. I don't think Eric will be so ugly about it. And you say he has no children? I think he may be excited. At least by the time you return to D.C., he will have processed his thoughts and will more likely give you the support you need for this pregnancy. Also, be certain to let him know your plans to return to D.C. I think that will make him happy."

I feel so deceptive right now, and all of this to save Shawnee's marriage and Elaine's life. There's nothing I can do to help Charise with that mess, though.

"Hmmm… I guess. Well, I know you have my best interest at heart, so I'll call," she said, still apprehensive.

"Sandy, I have an appointment coming in right now, so I have to get going. Call me later and let me know how it went," I said to push things along, although I had another ten minutes before my next patient was due.

"Okay, sis. Will do. Love you!" she said before hanging up.

Let's just hope all goes as hoped for. Eric will be happy about Sandy's baby and leave Shawnee alone before she has to confess to Robert or take legal action against Eric. Even more so, please let this baby belong to anyone but that sorry-ass Lewis. Bastard doesn't even take care of the ones he has.

15
Charise

I don't know what I was thinking when I agreed to carry this baby. Something about abortions doesn't sit well with me. Well, actually, it's that somehow I deluded myself into thinking I could really have something with my baby's daddy. When I told him I was pregnant, he seemed genuinely happy and remorseful that he couldn't be here for me through the pregnancy. He would call me at least once a day to check up on me and for phone sex. I even cut back on my one-nighters. Bitch needs some real dick from time to time. That phone shit just doesn't cut it for me.

Everything was going great until he told me that Sandy was also pregnant. He said he planned on leaving her to be with me, but now with that baby on the way, matters have been complicated. The last time we spoke, which has now been four weeks, he said Sandy was planning on returning to D.C. I haven't heard any more on the subject from anyone.

I finally received an email from Harmony in the form of an invitation. We are supposed to meet for dinner tonight. Perhaps then, I can gather some information. Since the announcement of my pregnancy, I seem to have been cut off. No one calls to check on me or returns my calls. I get generic emails from time to time, but nothing personal. I'm half tempted to pass on having dinner with them because I feel they have been treating me ugly as hell.

What the hell. I'm at the restaurant already. I may as well park and go in. Fifteen dollars for parking? I ought to make Harmony reimburse me for coming to this expensive-ass side of town.

When I arrived inside, I looked around for a familiar face. Finally, I saw Harmony walking towards me.

Wow, she's glowing. She actually looks happy. She must have found her a man.

She embraced me when she got to me. I wasn't too sure how to respond since I obviously knew her disappointment with my pregnancy, which showed on her face just as her eyes made contact with my bulging belly. I decided to hug her back.

"Good, you made it. The rest of us are in the back," Harmony said, motioning her arm in the direction for me to go.

"You seem to be glowing. Is that *happy* I spied on your face?" I asked as we walked to the secluded area of the 5-star restaurant.

"Well, I'd like to think I'm happy," she answered.

I wasn't too sure how to take that. Maybe I was just being paranoid, or maybe not. As we approached the table with all my sisters, minus Sandy, I could see the disdain on their faces as I approached. It was more obvious when they gave their half-ass waves as my greeting. I really wanted to cry and run out of there.

I don't need this shit. They always seemed to look down on me before this pregnancy, but this takes the cake.

I hesitantly sat down at the table, feeling some verbal lashings coming on.

To my surprise, Kelly asked, "So, Charise, how are you and the little one coming along?"

My paranoia responded, "Is that a loaded question?"

"Wow, aren't we a bit defensive this evening," Kelly stated, clearly put off by my response. "I was just simply asking a question, but never mind."

"Okay," Harmony jumped in, "we're getting off to the wrong start tonight. I would like for us to sit here and have a civilized dinner together, then I have some announcements to make, and then we will clear the air right before we probably get kicked out of the restaurant."

"Damn, do you think clearing the air would really get us put out of the restaurant?" Shawnee asked. "Why couldn't we have just met at your house?"

"Yeah," I agreed, still annoyed about the cost of parking.

"All in good time," Harmony responded. "For now, just put your orders in and let's eat."

"Sounds like a plan to me," Elaine chimed in. "I'm starving."

Through dinner, there wasn't much conversation. Wow! I must've really been missing something. Everyone seemed to have some tension.

After our meals and very limited conversation, Harmony began with, "As I mentioned earlier, I have some announcements. Do understand that they are non-negotiable. I am not here to get anyone's input or advice. Nor am I here to impart any advice.

"I have taken the liberty of assigning each of you with your own personal therapist. Lord knows each of you desperately need one. I will no longer be any of your personal therapists."

The look of horror was identical on each of our faces as we listened with open mouths, but speechless.

"I love every one of you, but I'm so sick of all your foolish antics weighing down my life, which leads to announcement number two. I have a For Sale sign at my home, and I am leaving D.C. in two weeks. When I think you all have gotten your drama under control, I'll send you a postcard with the address and phone number, but not a moment before then."

Elaine literally started choking. She wanted to say something, but couldn't speak.

Harmony sternly went on. "Good, the floor wasn't open for discussions at this point anyway."

I had never seen this side of Harmony. Heard about it from Shawnee and Sandy, but never saw it. She was absolutely cutthroat. I don't think she so much as blinked as her eyes scanned each of us.

"I will no longer keep any of your dirty little secrets, and if you have any, I suggest you either talk with your assigned therapist or God himself." Harmony motioned her hand as she pointed to the heavens. "For those of you who do not know, Sandy will be back in D.C. in three weeks, and she is equally as pregnant as Charise. They are two days apart in due dates." Harmony cut her eyes towards me, and all eyes followed. "I think it will be interesting to see who Lewis stands by when the time comes." She paused as though she just had an epiphany. "Oops! I think he has already made that clear since he's nowhere to be found."

We all looked at her in confusion. I was boiling inside. Harmony was being very insensitive.

"Yep! Lewis has disappeared on Sandy," Harmony continued. "He went to buy the proverbial pack of cigarettes, but not before clearing his clothes and important papers out. Just like the little bitch he is, he ran."

Now we were all shocked.

Lewis left Sandy? And he hasn't even contacted me? This can't be right.

"Oh, but have no fear for Sandy. She has another potential baby's daddy to help her through," Harmony said just before cutting her eyes toward Shawnee. Our eyes followed. "But, then again, he may not be available for Sandy either, because he was too pussy-whipped by the sister."

Now Shawnee choked. "Harmony!" was all she could get out.

Elaine's eyes bulged in horror. "NO! Not you, Shawnee?!"

"Let's not be hasty in passing judgment, Elaine, 'cause we know Shawnee wasn't the only one," Harmony said in a scary-pleasant, motherly tone. "And particularly when you didn't feel a need to inform your sister that your one and only trifling friend has been involved with her husband for months."

We were back to being confused. Which friend and whose husband? The answer came quick when Harmony's eyes went back to Shawnee.

Shawnee stuttered, "But, but, I don't understand. Whose husband and whose friend?"

"Elaine, should I do the honors, or would you like the floor right now?" Harmony asked Elaine.

"Harmony, how could you? I confided in you," Elaine rebutted.

"Actually, no, you didn't," Harmony said, shaking her head. "You left that lengthy-ass voicemail for anyone to hear while I was away on my trip."

"But I don't understand," Shawnee repeated, still looking confused.

"Damn, Shawnee, get a clue. She's obviously talking about Renee and Robert," Kelly sputtered. "That's so very fucked up, Elaine. As if it wasn't bad enough you were fucking Sandy's boyfriend slash baby's daddy, but you knew that trick-ass Renee has been fucking Robert and you didn't feel the need to let us know so we could whoop that bitch's ass?" Kelly shook her head furiously.

Shawnee finally found some words. "Okay, so would this have been before or after you felt the need to go tell Robert about my affair with Eric?" she asked, looking at Kelly.

"Don't be mad at me. I told you that punk was out there creeping. I was just trying to help you with that crazy-ass nigga you were creeping with. Let's see, that would be YOUR sister's man," Kelly retorted, folding her arms across her chest.

My mouth was wide open with disbelief. No wonder there was so much tension amongst everyone. I wanted to say something to those hypocritical bitches for ragging on me, but I knew I had better keep my mouth closed.

"And speaking of that crazy-ass nigga, Shawnee, Sandy was very unhappy to learn from him that you had already told him about Sandy's baby. See, when I foolishly talked Sandy into telling him about the baby, my way to get him to back off of you, she took my advice only to learn you beat her to the punch. So, imagine her confusion when she tried to figure out how you two knew each other enough to tell him something like that. She eventually figured it all out, but decided not to be mad at you because you didn't know initially about the two of them. However, that reasoning was short lived when she thought about your telling him about her baby. Matters were worsened when Eric professed his undying love for Shawnee to Sandy, but he said he will take care of the baby if it's his. Therefore, Shawnee, Sandy's going to kick your ass the first chance she gets," Harmony said with a smile. "Me? I'll be long gone from your madness."

Shawnee had tears in her eyes. All she could do was shake her head.

Cutthroat Harmony continued. "But, Elaine, before you think you're in the clear, Eric felt the need to confess his affair with you, as well. And as you already know, Sandy knows you knew about her and Eric's relationship. So, she plans on kicking your ass, as well."

I accidentally let out a brief laugh. Big mistake!

"Glad you find this amusing, Miss Charise, 'cause it was brought to Sandy's attention from Kelly that you're having a baby. Although Kelly kept secret your paternity, Sandy had me confirm her suspicions of Lewis fathering your child. Now she's thinking Lewis left her pregnant to run and be with you. She said she's going to fuck you up if she finds out he's with you," Harmony said to me with a raised eyebrow. "Needless to say, you have been completely disowned in her book. She wants nothing to do with you or the baby. She said you better pray she's not carrying Lewis' baby, as well."

Elaine stood up from the table. "Okay, I'm done here. I've heard enough. You can all kiss my ass."

"Ouch! That hurts, sis," Harmony said, amused. "But, I have just one more announcement before you go."

"I don't think I want to hear anymore. Particularly as you seem to be enjoying all of this," Elaine said, still standing.

"I'm sure you'll love this next one. It has nothing to do with any of you," Harmony said.

"I'm with Elaine on this. I don't think I want to hear anymore," Kelly added.

Shawnee was still looking catatonic as if her whole world just fell apart. I was somewhat relieved that everything was out, and I didn't have to feel like I needed to walk on eggshells around my holier than thou sisters.

"This is regarding your one and only brother, Angelo," Harmony put out there.

Oh Lord, what could Angelo have done and he's almost 3,000 miles away at UCLA? I was on the edge of my seat waiting to hear. From the looks of things, so were the others.

"Of course, you all know that you perfect and judgmental sisters don't make things easy for Angelo to talk about, so he has shared with me that he is gay. He doesn't want to come around any of us because he doesn't want any backlash of how he chooses to live his life. So, now I am telling you because I want whichever of you without blemish to cast a stone in Angelo's direction," Harmony dared.

Again, we were all shocked. Elaine fell back into her seat. Shawnee was at full attention with the news.

Kelly spoke. "Gay? But how? When? Oh my Lord! This can't be."

"Believe it! It is!" Harmony answered. She stood up and then announced, "Ladies, dinner is on me, and I hope you have enjoyed it as much as I have. I'll be in touch with each of your much-needed therapy contact information. And I'm out!"

With that, she walked off to pay the waiter and left the restaurant. The rest of us remained still trying to process it all.

I found something inside of me to finally speak up. I guess this must have been the "clear the air" portion that was about to get us thrown out the restaurant.

"You bitches have got a lot of nerve. You practically jumped on me when I told you about my pregnancy. All the while, you knew you were fucking Sandy's other dick on the side. Bitches!"

Elaine retorted, "First of all, I got your bitch, bitch. Secondly, I wasn't fool enough to carry any man's baby, especially one that my sister is currently married to. Thirdly, when I was fucking him WITH A CONDOM, I didn't know Shawnee was fucking him, too, or that Sandy was still fucking him. Unlike your dumb ass, who fucked a man UNPROTECTED that she knew was fucking her sister every day, you dumb-ass bitch!"

"Whoa! Whoa! Wait a minute," Kelly jumped in. "Don't talk to Charise like that. You didn't do everything with a damn condom, you ho. I guess you forgot who you told what to."

Just then, Shawnee got up without saying a word and left the restaurant.

Kelly continued on Elaine. "Your skank ass knew when you first saw that bastard at the club that was Sandy's dick, but it didn't stop you. Oh, but speaking of the club, you brought that bitch Renee to the club around us, when you knew she was fucking your sister's husband?" Kelly's voice was getting loud, and the ghetto was coming out.

"That's what you know," Elaine spat back. "I had no idea she was fucking Robert. I just learned that a few weeks ago. I tried to contact Harmony to figure out what to do."

"Bullshit!" Kelly yelled. "Why wouldn't you come tell me? You have no problem telling me every other piece of dirt." At this point, Kelly was standing as though she was ready to jump over the table and kick Elaine's ass. "You had to have gotten something out of the shit, because you wouldn't have kept that info to yourself. Why wouldn't you go to Shawnee? You were probably fucking him, too."

Elaine jumped up at Kelly, and there they were, fighting in the damn restaurant. I didn't know what to do; I wasn't going to jeopardize my baby to break them apart. It was probably my fault they were fighting. If I hadn't attacked Elaine and Shawnee, Kelly probably wouldn't have ended up involved.

Dishes were breaking. Shit was flying everywhere. People were screaming. And then came the inevitable: The police.

Harmony knew she was wrong to bring this anticipated disaster to a public restaurant. Then again, I guess she knew she didn't want the mess in her house. That's probably why she did things in the manner she did it.

It took six police officers to pull Kelly and Elaine apart. There must have been a couple thousand dollars worth of damage. I guess Harmony thought ahead by keeping us isolated from the main population of the restaurant. At first, I thought it was because of the nature of the conversation. Now I knew it was because she anticipated some physical activity, and she probably didn't want others to get hurt in the crossfire.

Now my sisters were being hauled off to jail, and I didn't have anyone to call. I already knew Shawnee and Harmony had turned their backs. I couldn't leave Kelly in jail. After all, she was in this mess for defending my honor. Elaine…I wouldn't mind leaving her ass, but at the end of the day, that's my sister. I didn't want anything bad to happen to her.

I guess I'll go bail the bitch out. I'm sure the restaurant is going to sue the shit out of both of them. Harmony ought to be the one paying for bringing this mess into these people's establishment, knowing what was to come.

I decided to try calling Harmony for the hell of it. Maybe she would actually feel some sense of responsibility.

"Hello," Harmony answered.

"Harmony, Elaine and Kelly are on their way to jail for fighting in the restaurant. Please, can you come and help? I can't deal with this by myself," I pleaded.

"Charise, they are grown-ass women, and if they don't know how to control themselves in a public place, which by the way is why I set the meeting in a public place, then it's time they learn control. Maybe a night or two in jail is just what they need. So, on that note, Charise, I suggest you go on home and have a good night. Bye-bye."

Before I knew it, Harmony hung up the phone.

Oh, Dear Lord, what do I do?

16

Elaine

I can't believe my ass is in jail. Fuck all those bitches. I'm done with each of them. And baby or no baby, I wish Sandy would get in my face. Damn, how did I end up fighting Kelly of all people? She and I were the closest of them all. I always sent business her way, and now here we both are locked the fuck up for fighting. That bitch-ass Charise is the one I should have been locked up for. I would have loved to kick that baby right out of her ass. Talking shit like she could actually kick someone's ass.

What makes it so bad is Kelly was right. I should have told her about Robert and Renee. I talked so much shit about Shawnee to Renee that I guess she felt I hated Shawnee. She told me how Mandingo went down on Shawnee in the club, after Kelly told me. I honestly didn't know Shawnee was having a full-blown relationship with the man. Somehow, Renee took that as her cue to go after Robert.

The gut kicker was when Renee asked me to partake in a ménage trio with this guy she had been kicking it with. She threw me for a big loop when she said the guy suggested me. So, I wondered who the hell she was dating that would know me without us having met. I have seen a couple of guys she was dating, and they didn't look too bad. So, my dumb ass agreed to it as long as I was paid well for it. I was told money was no object.

I should have known something was wrong when they insisted on the blindfolds and dark hotel room. But, I've dealt with the kinky, so I was like, *what the hell.* Besides, the price was alright.

Renee had blindfolded me and tied me to the bed with silk scarves. She had a variety of battery-operated toys on the nightstand and one large candle lit in addition to some smaller ones, but other than that, all lights were out. I ain't gonna lie. This kinky shit had me turned on big time. I was almost cumming just from the anticipation. The coolness from the air-conditioned room caused my nipples to harden. I was surprised because I didn't think Renee was capable of such. I was wondering if this ménage trio was really for her or for this mystery man. I always knew Renee was kind of clingy, but I didn't think she'd have it in her to be with another woman, let alone me.

Let the games begin:

I lie on the bed, blindfolded and tied to the bed while wearing red lace lingerie that had a matching red g-string. The outfit was purchased for me; expensive quality material that felt good against the skin. Renee wore a similar outfit in white. Of course, my outfit fit much more flattering than Renee's. Additionally, I was wearing my five-inch "come-fuck-me" pumps.

With all those toys I saw before being blindfolded, I was hoping the mystery man didn't turn out to be a mystery woman. Sure, I like to get my pussy sucked just as much as the next one, but Elaine prefers a good stiff dick with real blood pulsating through those veins. I don't want some toy dick as a substitute. I have done other couples, with women included, but I always need the dick as the main course.

It kind of surprised me that Renee had absolutely no words to speak to me. I was getting a little nervous about her strange, unusually quiet behavior, but then I figured she was just nervous about this threesome.

The few times I asked was she alright, she had answered with a high-pitched, "Yeah," which let me know she was lying. I also detected attitude. *Maybe she has a problem with her man's request for a ménage trio,* I thought.

I could feel the bed moving as she sat nervously waiting, shaking her leg. Then I heard the door open, and music came on. I wasn't too sure what that was all about. I could hear the sound of kissing. Slobbing was more like it. Just then, I felt thick, manly fingers rub my clit through the g-string before making their way to my breasts. My anxious breasts were fondled and then released from behind the lace fabric. Next came gentle sucking and licking. Damn, it was feeling good. It got even better when I felt those thick fingers playing at the door of my clit once again. Eventually, those fingers bypassed the g-string and found the entrance to my hot, wet cave.

Very briefly, when the sucking of my breasts stopped, I could hear more sucking. I assumed he was sucking on Renee's breasts at that point. Then a mouth returned to my breasts. Only it was a different mouth, less experienced. I cringed a little at the thought of it being Renee. That thought was confirmed when I heard her moan. I guess he was using his free hand to fuck her. As he fucked me masterfully with the fingers he had inside of my pussy, my moans drowned out the sound of Renee's moans.

Then everything stopped. I didn't know what was happening. Suddenly, I heard rummaging through the toy bag and then felt someone lie on the bed next to me. It smelled like Renee, although she doesn't wear any perfumes. I heard the noise from one of the toys, but still I didn't feel anything. Eventually, I heard Renee moaning again and felt her hand caressing my exposed breast. Then, out of nowhere, a hot mouth found its way to my wet pussy. I thought I was going to die. It felt so good. Next came the fingers in my asshole, just the way I like it. Whoever this mystery man was he knew just how to suck this pussy and turn me on. The tie binds were keeping me from running, so I had to just take it. Every time I tried to close my legs, he'd open them up again.

I could hear Renee getting off with her toys, and her sounds were unusually annoying to my ears. Almost pretentious. I hoped she didn't try to put that toy in me when she was done with it. That would've been so disgusting. Then Renee's tits were in my face. She was trying to get me to suck her breasts. I would have been able to resist, but with the way my pussy was being eaten, my mouth was wide open and receptive. Somehow, I actually got turned on. I could still hear Renee's toy working on her and could smell her pussy getting closer to my nose.

Damn! Renee straddled my face, with her pussy now at my lips. My hands were tied, so I couldn't even push her ugly ass off. No, what was worse is her fingers that were covered in her pussy juices were shoved into my mouth. I was eating Renee's pussy! Ain't that a bitch!

I guess I wasn't fulfilling her expectations, because I heard her say, "Come here, baby, and do me."

Isn't she the selfish one? All she's thinking about is her damn self, I thought.

I heard the mystery man whisper, "Turn around."

I wasn't too sure what that meant, but figured it out real soon. He had Renee reposition herself on me for a 69. Yep! Once again, I had Renee's pussy at my mouth along with her ass at my nose. Damn! I didn't sign up for that shit. Don't mind pussy, but not Renee's, and her pussy was super wet.

Renee wasn't trying to eat my pussy, just like I wasn't trying to eat hers. Lucky for her, mystery man helped her work on my pussy. I felt his fingers inside my pussy again and felt his breath on my inner thighs. Somehow, I got caught up in the excitement, and as a result, Renee became the beneficiary of some serious pussy eating on my part. For a brief moment, I didn't even care it was Renee. When she tried to lift her pussy away, my face lifted right with her. She was beyond ecstasy. She moaned and squirted big time.

I can't tell you at what point mystery man stopped touching me, but I figured he stopped when I felt his breath at my face as he joined me in eating Renee's pussy and ass. He supplied the fingers I was unable to supply for insertion into Renee's pussy, and then graciously gave me his fingers to suck on. Eventually, I heard Renee sucking, but it wasn't me being sucked. I heard some rummaging in the toy bag again while the sucking had ceased. Then a cold metal-like object made contact with my clit and started vibrating. I was like, "Whoa!" That caught me off guard, but it felt good. With my body jerking like a wild horse, Renee was unable to hold her position on top of me.

Again, everything stopped. I could hear the two of them moving around. I felt my knees lifted and spread by Renee, and once more, she half-ass attempted to eat my pussy, with the help of some other vibrating item. I then heard her scream out, and I could tell Renee was being fucked doggie-style while she worked on me. The problem with that was the more Renee got into the groove, the less effective she was becoming on me. After a mere couple minutes of them banging, he stopped. I heard a noise that sounded as if he had slapped her ass. Then I could hear him replacing the condom. Renee must have gone into the bathroom, because I could hear water running after the door closed.

There he was on top of me, sucking on my tits like it was the first time in his life he had seen breasts. His fingers were back in my pussy. He was groaning and moaning so much, I was wondering what was happening to him that had him grunting so. Then his mouth found my mouth, and his tongue was in the back of my throat. I tried to put up some resistance, but he wasn't having it. Finally, his dick made its way inside of me. Wasn't too big, but it felt damn good. He certainly knew how to use what he had to hit the right spots. His stroking techniques were very skillful. He was fucking me so good, I somehow got this mega strength that caused me to break one of the tie binds that confined me. That just turned him on more. He flipped me over and took me from the back, which was feeling so very good, but I was hoping he'd go for the asshole. That's the cherry on the top for me. He didn't quite get it, so I helped things along by using my free hand to give his dick guidance. At first, he kept moving my hand out the way, as he wanted his concentration to be on my pussy. Then he finally got the hint when my pussy was so wet, it kept causing him to slip out. Oh yes! He had arrived.

Wow! Renee better watch out 'cause I could see myself taking this one away from her, although he's supposed to be married, I thought.

Oh, he was fucking me properly. Oh, it was so, so good. My God, I lost count on how many times I climaxed!

After climaxing yet again, it occurred to me that I no longer heard any evidence of Renee in the room. I was about to lift the blindfold off, but his hand stopped me.

He said in my ear, "Leave it on for a few more minutes."

"Where's Renee?" I asked.

He answered, "She left. She's mad. She probably didn't like how good I was fucking you, and I still have some more for you. That asshole just turned me on even more. My dick is hard again," he whispered.

I didn't know what to think. What I do know is when I heard him say he had a hard dick for me again, I was like, *Fuck Renee! I get to have this dick all to myself.*

Then, still whispering, he said, "I'm going to turn you around, but I need you to keep the blindfold on. I'm going to take the other tie off your arms. I would like to eat your pussy some more and for you to taste me. Is that okay?"

"This is your lucky day, because I like sucking dick, and I

definitely love getting my pussy eaten," I seductively told him.

And there his dick was, in my mouth, and I sucked him as skillfully as his thirty-five hundred dollars was paying me to suck. He moaned. Damn near screamed. His mouth was vacuuming out every bit of juice he could find in my pussy. It was almost difficult to concentrate on sucking his dick. Then he stopped to change positions. He threw my legs up, holding onto my ankles, and was skillfully inside me once again.

He was doing great until I heard him say, "Oh, Elaine, you don't know how bad I wanted this pussy." He forgot to whisper that time.

That threw me. How bad he wanted me? Who was this man? Then I tried to place the voice. He sounded kind of nerdy. Almost like a black man who tries to talk like a white man. The dick was feeling good, but now it was hard to concentrate on getting my nut. I had to know who this man was pleasing me.

So, in the heat of passion, I intentionally pushed the blindfold up over my eyes. It still was hard to see with the low light from the one candle and my eyes readjusting from the blindfold. At that moment, he gave up his nut and plopped down on me with his face turned away from me. He laid there for a moment as his dick pulsated inside of my contracting pussy. Ooh, that was my favorite part of having a real dick inside of me. Well, that along with the hot explosion.

When he was able to collect himself, he got up to go to the bathroom. Just as he went into the bathroom and turned the light on, I caught a horrifying glimpse of Robert, my sister's husband.

Oh my Lord! What had just happened? I didn't know what to do or say. I moved the blindfold back over my eyes before he could realize I saw who he was. I could hear him in the bathroom washing up and talking to himself, saying, "Whew! That was some good pussy." He spoke lowly, as though he didn't want me to hear. "I got that pussy. You're the man."

My mind was racing. *What am I going to do? Why is Renee fucking my sister's husband and then including me in this madness? How could she do this to me? Do I confront his dumb ass? Do I just pretend I didn't know I was fucking him? How can I even tell on his ass without him telling on me? How can I tell on Renee's trifling ass now that she knows I also fucked Shawnee's husband? Damn her!*

Then Robert came from the bathroom. I lay silently, still not knowing what to say.

"I'm going to have to leave you now," he said, not even disguising his voice, as if someone wouldn't easily recognize his distinctive voice. "I would like for you to keep the blindfold on until after I leave. I wish we could do this again sometime, but it probably wouldn't be a good idea."

I was fuming. I just wanted him to hurry out before I got up the nerve to remove the blindfold and confront him. To add insult to injury, he came to the bed and kissed me again. I turned my head away.

"Okay, I guess that's my cue to get going."

I remained silent as he left. I didn't want to remove the blindfold and see the shit I had just done with yet another one of my sister's men. *What am I going to do?* I thought. To make matters worse, he had probably used my sister's income to pay for his indiscretions. I wondered how often he did that. I knew he didn't give Renee shit. She was just all too happy to be with her mystery married man, and she thinks it's ridiculous for a woman to accept money from a man for sex when he is equally pleasing her. To each his own, I say.

So now, I'm in jail behind this bullshit, and God help me when all the dirt comes out in the wash. Kelly put her finger right on it, but she won't give a damn that I was an unwilling participant. *Damn, what will happen if anyone finds out I have sex for money?* I haven't even confronted Renee because I figure she'd be all too happy to run and tell if I piss her off. I've been just avoiding her. She's pissed off anyway because her so-called man preferred fucking me instead of her. Ewww! And I ate that heifer's pussy.

I think when I open my New York City shoe boutique, I'm going to just live there and stay clear of my family. I have to make sure my D.C. staff will be able to run this boutique without me having to be around. When I do need to be around, I'll just stay incognito.

Damn, I have to get out of this jail. I have dicks to satisfy. They said we're going to be here all night. Thankfully, it pays to fuck the right people. I can't even call my sisters to get out of here, so I called one of my politically connected tricks who called his attorney. He said he'll have me out before the sun has fully risen.

Shit, I broke a nail fighting that damn Kelly. I don't wear that fake shit. It takes work to get my nails like they are. I'm sure the patrons from the restaurant had a field day when the straps to my top gave way, giving a free peepshow. Kelly probably pulled them intentionally. And I know damn well I felt those policemen cupping my tits as if they were trying to pull me and Kelly apart. If I'm not mistaken, one of them was a woman. I can't say I blame them, though. I'd want to feel my tits, too, if I were them. Hell, I get turned on looking at my body in the mirror every day. Nonetheless, I should have worn a bra, a sweater, or something more than what I had on. It was too cold outside anyway for this top. Better yet, I should have just put my jacket on and left when I was first planning to leave.

Should've, could've, would've!

17

Kelly

I know that damn Elaine fucked Robert. She absolutely lost it when I said that. How low can she go? What the hell? Did Renee tell her Robert had some good dick and she had to try it out for herself? I hope some of her store customers were in that restaurant, witnessing her tits popped out for the entire world to see. That's what she gets for wearing that skimpy-ass top with no bra when it's damn near winter.

Oh damn! Elaine is my biggest source of business. What will I do if she decides to cut me off? Shit! Shit! Shit! What have I done? Why would I go head to head with Elaine of all people? I should have whipped Harmony's ass for creating this disaster. Charise deserves an ass whipping just the same, but she's pregnant, so I'll leave that ass whipping for Sandy. That one, Charise will not get away from.

Poor Shawnee. She has got such a mess to deal with. She thinks I was wrong for talking to Robert about her affair with Eric. Maybe; but I was trying to help her get rid of that psycho. Especially when she told me that Eric informed her that he had Robert's job information and would be paying him a visit if she didn't come see him. And she fucked him again after all he has been putting her through. She was talking about she didn't have a choice. She had a choice to tell Robert herself and put an end to it once and for all. Maybe that was her excuse to go back and keep fucking him. Now that Robert knows, she can't use that as her excuse. But hold the presses! Robert's nasty ass has been fucking Renee of all people. I knew he was fucking somebody else other than Shawnee. Now I have to find a way to get the truth out of Elaine, 'cause after tonight, I know she fucked Robert, as well. That's just nasty. I don't know how I'll ever be able to look at her the same again.

Ugh! And my poor baby brother, Angelo. What the hell?! Gay? I need some answers. Is he the man in the relationship or is he the girl? Damn, did we turn him off from women? Or maybe we had too much influence, and he just wanted to be a girl, as well. Daddy would roll over in his grave to know his only son is also a girl. He still talks masculine on the phone, though. I don't know what thought is worse—him sticking his dick in another man's booty or another man sticking his dick in my brother's booty. Ugh! I can't think about it anymore.

And what's this shit with Harmony? She takes a mysterious vacation for a whole damn month, returns without telling anyone she's back, and now she's relocating to some mysterious part of the earth but we're not allowed to know where. That's some bullshit there! When we first arrived and I saw her glowing, I thought she went somewhere and found some dick. But, after the bullshit stunt she pulled tonight, it's obvious she was only glowing 'cause she knew the havoc she was about to wreak, and with her leaving, there's not a damn thing we could do about it. Nope, she can't have a man. A man makes you do nice shit, not mean shit like she did. Then she wants to tell us that she has a therapist for each of us to consult with. Again, that's some bullshit!

Wow! Sandy and Charise are expecting at the same time. What a joke. I hope Sandy is carrying Lewis' baby. That would be an interesting story for years to come. Oh no, the topper is that Lewis did a disappearing act. Dumb-ass Charise really thought Lewis was going to dump Sandy to be with her. I guess he found him another family to bust up. I wouldn't be surprised if he was right here in D.C. with his other kids' momma. I know he was still screwing her before he moved to Denver. I would have figured he was screwing her a few months back when he came, but apparently, that's when he was screwing Charise.

It would be equally interesting if Sandy is carrying Eric's baby, and Shawnee is still sleeping with him. See, although Robert tried to play that mad shit when I told him about Eric, he acted like he was going to forgive her and stay by her side. He just couldn't fuck her anymore without him getting crept out behind her having been with another man. Shawnee vowed never to speak to me again. Oh, but now she has the real story. Not only has Robert been having an affair, but it's with the very person Shawnee despises. I'm sure the plot will thicken once the truth about Elaine's involvement with Robert comes to light, and I know there's some involvement.

Boy, am I going to kick Charise's ass for being the cause of me getting locked up. She actually started the shit with Elaine and Shawnee. I should have stayed out of it and let Elaine whip Charise's ass. Now all my business contacts are all fucked up. I have to find a way to fix this shit with Elaine.

Damn, when you get all the way down to it, this whole shit is my fault. If I would have kept our lame asses at the jazz club and never went to Megaplex, none of this would have happened. Well, except the part about Charise fucking Lewis.

Man, my back is killing me. It probably got hurt when I fell on that table. I guess I better try getting comfortable in this cell. They said we won't see the judge until morning. This is fucked up on so many levels.

18

Shawnee

"Why are you sitting here in the dark?" Robert asked when he finally strolled in at 12:30 a.m. and saw me sitting in the living room.

I couldn't answer. I was still too numb from the news I had just learned. I couldn't even cry because I was having difficulty processing how Robert's infidelity would leave him with my sister's best friend. I still needed answers, but couldn't speak to ask any questions.

So he repeated, "Shawnee, why are you sitting in the living room with the lights off? Why didn't you just go to bed?" He walked over to me when I still wouldn't answer. "Are you alright? Has that guy done something else to you?" he asked, referring to Eric all too gladly.

I finally found some words. "Robert, it would be in your best interest if you leave right now."

"Leave?" he asked, looking confused. "Where am I going? You're the one who probably wants to leave," he said all smug. "Are you expecting company? I don't think I should be leaving for that. You should."

"The only company I expect if you don't leave is the Medical Examiner's office to come collect your dead body. Them and the police to take me away," I responded.

"What the hell?" he said, confused. "Are you threatening my life? Shouldn't that have been my response when your sister told me about that jerk who started stalking you when you tried to end your affair?"

Oh, how I wanted to strangle Kelly for telling Robert about Eric. I somewhat understood where she was coming from, but I should have been able to do it my own way. And with a little time, I wouldn't have had to say a word, given Robert's affairs.

Eric's stalking was getting worse. I knew something had to be done once he recited Robert's work information to me. He planned on paying Robert a visit. So, I went back and slept with him again just to buy some time until I could figure out what to do. Kelly decided to figure it out for me and went to Robert herself. Trying to be Mr. Reasonable, he forgave me for my actions. He even accepted part of the responsibility for putting his work before his marriage.

He wasn't so forgiving that he would intimately touch me again, though. He won't even cuddle with me in bed. He says he's just turned off right now, knowing another man has "handled" me. He believes eventually that feeling will fade, and we can get back some sense of normalcy in our marriage. He even recommended we go to marriage counseling, but of course, his busy work schedule hasn't permitted any time.

I started accepting what Kelly was saying about Robert cheating on me, but a couple of times when I actually called him at the office late at night, he and many other colleagues were there working. So, I discounted the notion of him cheating on me. He would even be so kind as to call and let me know when he and some of his colleagues were going out for a drink after work. I appreciated him for telling me, because I did want him to have some kind of social life outside of work and marriage. That social life wasn't supposed to include other women, though, and it certainly wasn't supposed to include that damn Renee.

What I would like to know is how long they were together. Did she get her cue that night she saw Eric on me in the club? Or was it that she was with him before then? Whatever the case, Robert has met Renee on many occasions. He also knew she was Elaine's friend and how much I didn't like her. So, that's who he chooses to have an affair with. One thing is obvious; something's been going on for longer than the amount of time Robert knew about Eric.

A divorce with Robert will most certainly be a messy one. We have a lot of assets tied up together. We both have high salaries. The fight over the assets would be the cause for astronomical attorney fees. Well, for me that is. Robert wouldn't have attorney fees. Then I'd have to find a way to prove that he was cheating on me long before I cheated on him. I need to find out from Elaine how long Robert and Renee have been seeing each other. That would help a lot.

"You know what Robert? I'm just going to let it go. I don't even want to talk about anything with you." I stood up to go upstairs. "Goodnight."

Robert stood looking perplexed. He was at a loss for words. I guess he didn't know whether to push the issue with me to find out what was going on or just let it go. He chose the latter.

When he arrived in the bedroom, looking as though he was about to get comfortable, I warned, "I don't think you want to sleep in here with me. You'd probably be a lot safer in another room of the house."

He gave me the "WTF" look, but then took heed without any further exchange of words. As he was gathering some items from his drawer and the closet, I could hear him mumbling. He was talking big shit under his breath, but he wasn't stupid enough to make any of it audible.

I decided to back off so I could gather more facts against him. He was neglecting me long before my affair with Eric, which probably means his affair has been going on as long as he's been neglecting me; if not with Renee, certainly with others. I'll call Elaine in the morning.

Maybe I'll get some kind of info.

I am still rattled by Harmony. What has come over her? At least I know not to tell her shit ever again. I'm certainly not looking forward to an encounter with Sandy. Maybe I'll divorce Robert and do like Harmony is doing—relocate to a destination unknown to the family. We have an office in New York, Houston, Chicago, and Los Angeles. I could pick any of them to transfer to. D.C. cold is cold enough for me, so I don't know if I could handle Chicago cold.

First, let me get to the bottom of this Robert and Renee affair. Then I'll work everything else out from there.

19

Charise

I could hear the phone ringing as I turned the key in the door. By the time I reached the phone, it stopped ringing. The caller ID displayed the words "Unknown Caller".

This is crazy. I'm pregnant and alone. Right now, I need a man by my side. I can't remember the last time I had a dick up inside of me. The blowjob I gave the guy I met last week doesn't count because once he came in my mouth, he couldn't get his dick back up again. I just sent his stupid ass on home.

I found his behind sitting at a bus stop in the cold rain. He looked alright…fuckable…so I picked him up and gave him a ride. Since he wasn't in any rush, I brought him to my place to warm him up and get my pussy some attention. After I sucked him off, all of a sudden he got a conscious, telling me that his girl at home was also pregnant, which was making it difficult for him to be with me. He wouldn't even play with my pussy, eat it, or anything. He had to go.

I don't feel like I have anyone to talk to. Tonight was a mess in the restaurant, and to make matters worse, now I have to do battle with Sandy in a few weeks. Why doesn't she just stay her ass in Denver? If she would have given Lewis the boot when we let her know about his advances, none of this mess between the sisters would be happening. Lewis would not have been around to keep making passes at me. She would not have had a need to go to Denver, leaving the Elaine and Shawnee debacle to then come next. Now all the damage is done, so why bother returning to D.C.? Oh yeah, I forgot. Lewis left her ass pregnant with her fourth child, and she needs her family to dump her children off on while she finds another man. The typical Sandy move. This time, she won't have Harmony to dump her kids on since Harmony is leaving.

The phone rings again with an unknown caller. Typically, I won't answer any unknown calls, but I keep hoping to hear from my baby's daddy again. So, I answer.

"Hello?"

"Hey, sexy, you miss me?" the voice said.

"Who is this?" I asked

"Damn, how many niggers do you have calling you sexy that you should be missing?" he asked.

I was pretty certain it was Lewis, but didn't want to mess up if it wasn't.

"Well, I'm going to hang up now if you want to play games," I responded.

"Charise! I thought you like playing games on the phone. I know you like to rub the phone all over that fat pussy when I talk nasty to you," he said, chuckling. "So how's our baby coming along?"

I came to life and lit up like a Christmas tree.

"Hey, baby! I miss you so much. You don't know how much I wish you were here with me right now. Everything has been so crazy. I heard you left Sandy," I rambled on without taking a breath.

"Yeah, I told you I would. It's going to be you, me, and our baby forever," Lewis said.

"Baby, are you serious?" I asked almost like a five-year-old.

"Serious as a heart attack. What do you think about moving here to Denver?" he asked.

"Denver?" I gasped. "Why would I want to move to Denver?"

"Sandy's planning on moving back to D.C., and I figured it would be too much drama there with both of you having my baby. You're the one I want to be with," Lewis reasoned. "I can't get enough of that fat ass of yours."

I was grinning from ear to ear. "Lewis, I have something to tell you."

Here comes the start of World War III.

"Sandy is carrying another man's baby, not yours."

"What did you say?" he asked, annoyed.

"I just found out tonight. Apparently, while you were with me, she was with one of her ex-boyfriends," I told him.

"Where did you get that from?" he asked.

"From my sisters. Supposedly, she confided in them. I think that's why she was planning to return to D.C., so she could be with him," I answered.

I know I'm wrong, but this will help me get Sandy out of the picture for good. I can have Lewis all to myself. And he wants me to come to Denver to be with him.

Lewis got quiet, so I called out, "Lewis, are you there?"

He stuttered. "Yeah…yeah…yeah, sexy, I'm here. I'm just trying to digest what you just told me." He then said, "Yeah, I made the right decision when I picked you. You're loyal to your man. I need that."

He knows all the right things to say. I don't know about living in Denver, though.

"Baby," I said.

"Yeah, what's up?"

"Can we be together any place other than Denver? It's too cold there," I pled.

He chuckled. "It's not that bad. You can handle it. It's actually beautiful here."

"Still, that's your and Sandy's town together. I want to go someplace where it's warmer and where we can make our own memories together," I told him.

Again, he chuckled. "Okay, I'll work on a different place then. So you'll be okay with whatever I choose, right?"

"Yes, baby," I answered. "I'll just be happy that we're together, as long as it's not in Denver.

We both laughed.

I was lying in the bed on my back, feeling on top of the world.

"Baby, please don't take so long to call me next time. I was getting stressed out," I told him.

"I'm sorry. I had to figure out things on my end, and with Sandy telling me she was expecting, it just complicated matters. But, now that you tell me she's expecting some other dude's kid, things just got less complicated. As soon as I get another cell phone, I'll give you the number. I don't want to make any move that gives Sandy any rights. Right now, if I get a cell phone with a contract, she'll get a record of my calls somehow. It's just too much drama," Lewis said.

"Honey, I miss you. The baby is growing, my tits and butt are getting bigger, and you're missing it," I expressed like a whiney kid while rubbing between my legs. "Can you fly in and come see me for a couple of days?"

"I can do better than that. I can be there in about an hour. I'm in Baltimore at my boy's house. I could have been there already, but I couldn't reach you," he answered.

YES!

"Oh, baby, you've just made my day! I'll be looking for you," I responded.

"See you then," he said before hanging up.

This is just what the doctor ordered. I could even feel the baby moving as though he or she just got happy. My man is coming to see me, and I'm about to get some damn good dick up in this pussy. Not only that, but he wants us to be together. I guess the better woman ended up winning in the end.

20

Harmony

Alright, so maybe I was wrong for doing what I did, but it sure felt damn good to get all of their nonsense off my shoulders. The look on all their faces was priceless. I wish I had the whole thing on video so I could watch it over and over when I need a good laugh. And the fight between Elaine and Kelly…if only I could have been a fly on the wall for that. Let me stop laughing. I probably can't show my face back in that restaurant again because of them. Oh well, I'm moving soon anyhow.

I'm flying back to Houston tomorrow. I decided to get an apartment instead of a house. I figure if things actually work out for Todd and I, we'd have one house too many. If it doesn't, then I could take my time finding the house that I want when I know the areas better.

I'm definitely looking forward to spending time with Todd. He made the last two trips here to D.C. I don't know how much longer I'll be able to hold out sexually. Just being around him causes my hormones to rage. He says he's okay with waiting as long as I want to. I'm trying to take a page out of Kelly's book, with the waiting period. She makes a good point about getting to know the man you give your body to.

The entire time we spent in Mexico, I was waiting for Todd to show some sign of sexual frustration, to gauge his ability to actually hold out. He was perfect. He didn't push the issue one time. At one point, I wondered if he had a swarm of women, but I guess if they were anything significant, they would have been sharing his vacation rather than me. When I asked why he was single, he told me that he only seems to meet women who come in as patients, and he would never allow himself to get caught up with his patients. He also said he works a lot to occupy his time, so that leaves him single.

We had two bedrooms in our suite in Cancun, and each night, he graciously returned to his own room. That made him all the more attractive to me. Each time he came to D.C., he retired to my guest bedroom without any pressure. The truth is I want him more each time, but I will at least hold out until I finish my relocation. Just two more weeks, and I will be done with D.C. for good.

21
Kelly

I couldn't believe Elaine invited me over to her place. To be honest, I'm a little scared of what she has in store for me. Maybe she wants to finish up the fight from last week.

I was happy when the restaurant agreed to drop the charges as long as Elaine and I paid the $9,000 fine. I wasn't too happy with the amount, but it beats being in jail and having a criminal record that would have made us pay restitution anyway. I have to give kudos to Elaine's attorney who worked that deal out. My attorney wasn't worth a damn. I guess Elaine wants to see me so she can bully me into paying her $4,500 share and attorney fees. That would be classic Elaine, the money-hungry bitch.

When I arrived, she greeted me with a hug. Scary! I returned the hug.

"Thanks, sis, for coming," Elaine said, seeming genuine.

"I will admit I was very reluctant," I replied, still nervous.

"I understand," she said. "Can I get you something to eat or drink?"

Lord knows I was both thirsty and hungry, but fear wasn't going to let me accept anything.

"No thanks. I'm fine," I lied.

We made it to her living room and sat across from one another. My eyes surveyed my surroundings for any sign of weapons. The two machetes hanging over her fireplace only increased my fear.

"Take it easy, Kelly." Elaine spied my concern. "I'm not going to attack you or anything. Actually, I wanted to give you this."

She picked up a folded paper and handed it to me. I gasped when I saw it was a check for $4,500.

"Elaine! What…what is this?" I stuttered

"I felt as though I owed you that. You shouldn't have had to pay that fine. The fight was my fault, and I'm accepting responsibility."

Just like her ass to want to show somebody up. She just had to be the bigger one and make me feel like shit.

"No, Elaine! I can't accept this. The fight was just as much my fault. I shouldn't have stood up in your face saying all those mean things," I said, determined not to let her be the bigger one.

"Well, you might feel differently after I tell you what I have to tell you," she responded.

Guilt?! Elaine is paying out of guilt? This should be interesting.

"I'll bite. What's the deal?" I asked, curious.

Elaine looked nervous as hell. She started fidgeting with her hands, and then began. "You were on to something when I jumped up at you, but it's not quite the way you probably think it is."

Elaine fucked Robert! I knew it! I knew it!

"Go on," I encouraged, now sitting on the edge of my seat.

"I slept with Robert without knowing it, and I didn't feel I could talk to anyone about it," she responded.

Okay, how does someone fuck someone without knowing it? I could feel my anger rising.

"You know, Elaine, maybe this isn't a good time to talk about this," I warned, shaking my head. "I don't think I have the capacity to process this right now."

"Please, Kelly, just hear me out," Elaine pled with tears in her eyes. "This has been killing me, and I couldn't even talk to Harmony about it. Trust me, it's not how you think."

"You're right, because I can't think of how two people can have sex without knowing it," I harshly answered, forgetting my fear.

The tears were pouring from Elaine's eyes.

Elaine doesn't cry. Wow, this is some serious shit. Alright, let me try to be objective.

"I'm sorry," I said. "Tell me what or how this happened."

When Elaine composed herself, she began to tell me of the trio and the blindfold adventure. She said she had absolutely no idea Robert was the man Renee was creeping with. She also told me that she never confronted either of them for fear of what the ramifications to the family would be.

While my heart goes out to my sisters who are victimized by this bullshit, my blood is boiling. I'm going to beat Renee's ass, and we are going to fix Robert if it's the last thing I do.

"Why would that bitch call herself your friend and do this to you?" I demanded. Before she could answer, I said, "I'm going to fuck her up, Elaine. You know I can't stand that bitch. Renee will not get away with this shit, and Robert is going to pay dearly."

"Shawnee has been trying to reach me, and I've been avoiding her. I don't even know what to say to her," Elaine said.

"Tell the truth! She has a right to know. That freaky bastard is walking around like he's God Almighty, issuing out forgiveness, while he knows what he has done and been doing. Oh, he's going to pay!" I was pacing back and forth in anger. "I know Harmony doesn't want to hear shit, but I think she needs the whole story, as well. See, right now, you're looking like a cutthroat bitch, when actually it's not you at all."

"Gee thanks!" Elaine chuckled through tears. "Well, there's one detail I left out that I'd like to hold back as best as possible, but I think it's important to Shawnee."

"Oh Lord! I don't know if I can handle more," I said dramatically, while sitting back down on the sofa. "Go on!"

"Robert paid thirty-five hundred dollars for that ménage trio. When Renee asked me for the ménage trios and offered the money, I was game. Still, I didn't know it was Robert. When I actually saw it was him, I was pissed off by the fact that he's using Shawnee's money to pay for his indiscretions. I wonder how often he does this," Elaine explained.

"Damn, at least I know how I can find a couple extra dollars when I'm running low on cash," I joked under the circumstances. "Wow, I didn't know guys are so hard up for sex that they'd pay like that." I paused and had a thought. "Hold up. I know Shawnee has some freaky ways about her, so why would Robert want to go elsewhere? And to her sister, no less?"

"Maybe that was his own sick, freaky fantasy," Elaine answered. "I remember his nasty ass saying to me that he wanted me for a long time. That was the giveaway that made me know something was wrong. I still wasn't certain until I saw him entering the bathroom. I wanted to die right at that moment. Especially when he said he wished we could do it again sometime."

"You should have gotten up and beat his ass right then. My back is still fucked up from last week," I said, rubbing my back, "but I know you could have hurt his nerdy ass. I can't believe you didn't pick up on that nerdy voice of his."

"I started to, but then dismissed that notion when I thought about it being someone Renee was involved with. Never in a million years would I have thought Renee was capable of such. Hell, I didn't think she had it in her for a ménage trio," Elaine answered.

"Ewww! I just had a horrible vision. Please tell me you didn't do it to Renee. Ugh! Please no!" I pled with Elaine.

"Imagine how I feel. Please don't remind me," she said, defeated.

"Oh, Elaine! I don't know what's worse: fucking Robert or doing it to Renee's ugly ass. Hell, at least Robert is nice looking. Nerdy, but nice looking. But, Renee? That bitch has boils and craters on her face. I can only imagine what below looks like," I said, dramatizing. "Oh, I think I'm going to be sick."

"Well, I've heard your stomach grumbling since you got here. You're probably sick from hunger," Elaine laughed. "I guess you were afraid that I was going to poison you or something?"

I laughed uncontrollably. She had hit that nail right on the head.

"Fuck you!" Elaine laughed again.

22

Elaine

Kelly and I decided to call Shawnee over and tell her everything. I couldn't let on that the "play for pay" was a way of living for me, so I acted like it was a one-time favor to Renee.

God knows it was a huge weight lifted off my shoulders to finally tell of the fiasco. I have done some low shit in my life, but I would have never intentionally had sex with my sister's husband. I guess it is low as hell that I actually enjoyed it very much. That detail I'll keep to myself, though. I also kept the anal sex part to myself when I heard Shawnee bitching about him not doing her, leaving her half done when they do fuck.

After Kelly and I did all we could to console Shawnee, we plotted the destruction of both Renee and Robert. Since neither was aware of the knowledge we had, we were one up on them. Ironically, Renee hasn't made one attempt to contact me since that night. She probably realized Robert used her ugly ass to have an opportunity to fuck me, and she damn sure wouldn't want me to know that. She's also probably wondering if I learned Robert's identity after she left. She has to be wondering why I made no attempt to call her just the same.

So the plot begins:

I called Renee at work. I knew she'd answer.

"Renee, we have a problem. I need to see you and your boyfriend," I said.

"Well, Elaine, this really isn't a good time to get into this. I'm at work," she responded uncomfortably.

"Then, obviously, it must be very urgent if I'm calling you at work. You know I wouldn't bother you at work."

"What is this all about? What's so urgent?" she asked with irritation in her voice.

"I need to see both of you. We could do the blindfold in the dark if you don't want me to see him, but we all have to talk. ASAP!" I urged. "Tell me when we can meet."

"Well, I can't do that, Elaine!" Renee answered, agitated. "I haven't heard from the asshole since that night." Her voice was indignant. "But, I'm sure that's just how you wanted it."

"What?!" I gasped, but wasn't really surprised. "Renee, what are you talking about? I wasn't trying to interfere with your relationship. You're the one who asked me for the ménage trios. I didn't feel comfortable with the whole arrangement."

"What do you need to tell me? I'm working," Renee snapped.

"I need to find the guy, Renee. I'm pregnant. He didn't use a condom," I partially lied. "Could you at least have him call me? We need to talk about this. You know I'm against abortions."

"Elaine, what the fuck do you want from me? I told you I haven't spoken to him. I saw him put on a condom before I left. If you allowed him to fuck you without a condom, then it sounds like your problem. Leave me the fuck out of your shit!" she yelled.

I had to contain my laughter. I could just imagine everyone in her neighboring cubicles all in her business.

"But, Renee," I tried to sound as if I were crying, "please don't do this to me and my baby. I am in this predicament because I was doing you a favor. I could find him myself if you both didn't leave me blindfolded and tied up in a hotel room. I need you to get in touch with him and have him call me. I'm at home right now. Please, Renee. Otherwise, we could meet at a hotel or something." I made sobbing noises.

Thankfully, I had Kelly and Shawnee's phone extension on mute, because they were cracking up at my performance.

"Fine, Elaine. I'll call him at work and have him call you. He's probably going to block his number, so be sure to answer," she conceded. "And one more thing, I'm sorry for dragging you and a helpless baby into this mess, but leave me the fuck alone from now on! I got a new man, and I ain't got time for none of your shit."

Then she slammed down the phone's receiver.

"A new man? Doesn't she have a lot of damn nerve? Now I guess we just wait," I said to Shawnee and Kelly.

"I would love to hear the conversation when she calls his ass. She's probably going ballistic on him," Kelly said.

"Did he really fuck you without a condom?" Shawnee asked sadly, ignoring everything else.

"He used a condom. I could hear when he was changing it. I could also feel it. Didn't you hear Renee say she saw him put it on?"

Again, I partially lied. I didn't actually feel it, and I only heard him change it that one time. I also felt his hot volcanic explosion that had me tightly squeezing my legs for days after. I know for certain he didn't have one on when I was sucking his dick. That's too much information to give up to Shawnee, though.

"What I want to know is how this ugly bitch got a new man already?" Kelly asked with attitude. "I mean, I just don't get how niggas are lining up to fuck her ugly ass."

"I don't know, but she never had a problem getting one. Most of them are cute. I'd look at them and wonder how myself. Leave it to her, she thinks her pussy is gold, and smart men know what's good for them," I answered.

"Stop it! You both are making me sick. The thought of that bastard putting his little pecker inside of me after having been with that nasty bitch…" Shawnee said, disgusted.

Hell, I enjoyed that little pecker myself. It ain't always what they got, but how they use it. Then again, I've learned how to get off on some of my tricks with a dick no bigger than a pinky. Perhaps the skills don't lie with the man, but with the woman.

Ten minutes later, my phone was ringing. I decided to let the voicemail pick it up in hopes that he would be dumb enough to leave a message. He was.

"Hi, Elaine," he said in that nerdy-ass voice. "I just received a very vulgar message from your friend Renee on my voicemail. She said you were pregnant with my child. We need to discuss this because I am a happily married man, and I can't have any illegitimate children. If it's money that you need, then let me know. Under no circumstance can you have this baby. Name your price to make this happen. Please call me as soon as possible on my private phone…301-555-7080. I'll be waiting for your call. Also, I want you to know that I'm very sorry this happened. I think you're a very beautiful woman, and under different circumstances, I would love nothing more than to stay by your side and raise this child with you. But, that's just not realistic. So, again, name your price. That's about as fair as I can be to you at this time. You deserve much better. Believe it or not, I actually have feelings for you. Renee and I are no longer involved because of my feelings for you, but I guess none of that matters to you or the baby. I guess I should have been more careful. I also wish I didn't have to blindfold you, because I would have loved to look into your beautiful eyes when I made love to you. It was love for me, but unfortunately, like I said before, I'm happily married and plan to stay that way."

I had to grab Shawnee, who was furiously in tears, when she was going to reach for the phone. I wanted him to keep digging his own grave.

He continued. "I truly wish there were a way I could make love to you again, but that's not possible without there being major complications. Do know, being with you was everything and more than what I'd hoped for. Again, call me so we can talk…301-555-7080. Talk to you soon," he said, then hung up.

Shawnee screamed out like someone was killing her. Kelly and I tried to console her. Thankfully, he mentioned the blindfold, because that helped my story.

Shawnee went into the bathroom a sobbing fool.

"Okay, time for the truth," Kelly said to me as soon as Shawnee was securely in the bathroom.

"Huh?" I was puzzled.

"You did not feel a damn condom on his dick. You can tell that lie to Shawnee, but you're not going to tell that lie to me," she demanded quietly to keep Shawnee from hearing.

"What was I going to say, Kelly? Do you think I wanted to tell anymore lies to Shawnee? You saw her. What should I have said to her?" I asked.

"I guess you're right, but you better hope she doesn't figure it out as easily as I did. He damn near admitted he didn't use a condom in the message. If she listens a few more times, she's going to pick up on it, Elaine," Kelly warned.

I just shook my head in disgust and started crying myself.

"Tell that bastard you need fifteen thousand dollars to abort the baby," Shawnee demanded when she came out of the bathroom looking like a wounded raccoon. "And don't you dare tell me any more fucking lies! You knew damn well he wasn't wearing a condom when you told me that bullshit lie."

All I could do was cringe. I expected her to jump on me at any second, but Kelly calmed her down.

"Shawnee, Elaine was just trying to spare you further hurt. Don't be angry at her. She was the victim here, as well," Kelly reasoned.

"I know. You're right, but it hurts like hell!" Shawnee yelled, foaming at the mouth while she spoke. "How dare that sick bastard carry on about how happily married he is, but go on about how he made love to Elaine and wanted her so bad. BASTARD! I don't even know that number he left," she cried out.

Now we were all crying.

"I say go for twenty thousand, and slap him with divorce papers at the time of the payoff. Make sure that punk doesn't get to leave with shit beyond the clothes on his back," Kelly suggested.

"I agree," I added.

When we composed ourselves, we put the plan into motion, and Robert went for it.

23

Shawnee

This sneaky bastard has over seven million dollars in a secret bank account that I knew nothing about. On top of that, he has a few hundred thousand in four other accounts and more in an offshore account. I should take him for half of it all, but at this point, I just want him gone sooner than later. Fighting for his assets would only prolong a divorce. I understand that's his money and he had a life before we hooked up, but I'm sure I'd be entitled to something for my aggravation. I wish I would have known this shit when I let Elaine tell him twenty thousand. I guess that was a drop in the fucking bucket for his sad ass.

I was glad when my attorney said it wasn't extortion since Robert was on tape saying he was willing to pay any price. It was decided the twenty thousand dollars would be punitive damages for Elaine since she too was victimized. The divorce papers I had drawn up states Robert will walk away with his personal assets, his car, and nothing more from our marriage. Unfortunately, I had those bitches drawn up before I knew about the millions. I should have just had his ass taken out and collected it all.

My attorney also said Robert wouldn't be able to prove my own indiscretions without Kelly. Furthermore, I have his entire confession on Elaine's voicemail tape, along with the three copies made. Robert being caught on video making the payoff was the icing on the cake. He left another dumb-ass message on Elaine's voicemail saying he was leaving the money in a mailbox at The UPS Store, with a pickup time, and this time, he added, "I love you," before hanging up. He had the key sent to her store by messenger. His fool ass used the store next door to the building he works in. Elaine knows full well he works in that building. Then he was caught on camera spying on her as she made the pickup.

With my divorce attorney, comes a damn good private investigator that also caught him soliciting prostitutes—common streetwalking bitches at that. On the voicemail for the number he left Elaine, his fool behind identifies himself as "Joe," but the phone number is actually registered to him. Being the resourceful wife that I am, I was able to obtain a copy of the phone records for that phone. There were two numbers on there that were kind of frequent, and one of those had been listed on the records for at least six months. The others seem to be recent. Renee's number didn't pop up until July, which was after our night at the Megaplex. The bitch probably went skipping off to Robert to tell what she saw that night when Mandingo had his face between my legs.

Ironically, Renee never got more than a Happy Meal or a Scooby snack from Robert. I guess his target was Elaine all along when he got involved with that bitch Renee, who still has something coming her way from me.

Robert's last night in my house went like this:

It was the following Friday night after Elaine picked up her money. Elaine and Kelly were over while we packed all of Robert's shit in boxes. Robert came strolling in as usual at 12:30 a.m., pretending to have been working so hard. I had Elaine and Kelly park their cars out of Robert's view. When he brought his happy-go-lucky ass in the house, he spied the boxes.

"Hey, what's up with the boxes?" he asked with a stupid smile still on his face.

"Oh, we're just packing up some shit," I answered.

"We?"

"Yeah, I had my sisters to come help me," I answered as nicely as I could. "Come here. Join me on the sofa. I was watching this hilarious video. I would love for you to see it." I patted the sofa beside me and hit the remote for the DVD player.

He reluctantly came and sat next to me. "But I don't understand. Why are your sisters upstairs packing stuff?"

"Oh, don't worry about them. They're just packing stuff I don't need in this house anymore. Come on and let's watch," I said.

He jumped up immediately when he spotted himself watching Elaine make the pickup.

"Oh, come and sit. It gets even better," I teased.

He wouldn't sit. "I demand to know what's going on, Shawnee," he said, trying to sound tough.

"If she doesn't want to tell you, I'll be glad to tell you, Robert," Kelly chimed from behind, coming down the stairs with another box in tow. "You're leaving, and there ain't a damn thing you can do about it."

"What? What is this all about?" he stuttered.

"Why don't we ask Elaine," Kelly said. "Elaine! Could you come here for a minute? You shouldn't be working too hard anyway. You might hurt the baby." Kelly kept a straight face, looking Robert directly in the eye while she spoke as if she'd jump him any second.

Elaine came downstairs carrying an envelope. She handed it to Robert.

"What's this? Why are you here?" Robert asked, terrified while taking the envelope. He tore into it and saw the divorce papers. "What?

What is this?" he asked again.

"Need a pen, motherfucker?" I asked.

"Sister-fucker is more like it," Elaine corrected.

"I don't know what you're talking about," he lied.

"Kelly, give him the other envelope," I directed Kelly.

She picked up another envelope from the table and handed it to Robert. Again, he tore into the envelope. He saw ultrasound photos of a baby that had the name "Wiggins" typed on the side.

"Oh my gosh. But you said you were going to abort the baby," Robert said to Elaine. "I paid you what you wanted. Why are you doing this?"

"You couldn't pay me enough to make me kill any baby of mine, Robert," Elaine said. "Just sign your damn divorce papers, take your shit, and be gone from our lives for good."

"Oh, and just so you know, Robert, I have cameras all around recording every bit of our conversations," I lied. "Sign the papers, and this won't have to get any uglier and embarrassing for us than it already is. I'm keeping this house and all the contents. You get to walk away with your personal assets, all of your hidden bank accounts, and your car, in addition to 'Joe's' cell phone. If you want to drag this out, we'll start exploring those other bank accounts that allow you to pay for your mistresses. Speaking of accounts, the joint accounts are empty and the credit cards are cancelled. So don't even think about those. The way I see it, I was entitled to your portion of what you put in those accounts."

"Shawnee, you can't do this. What about your affair? I forgave you," he said matter-of-factly.

"What affair? When did I have an affair, Robert?" I yelled.

"Kelly knows. You had an affair, too," he said, getting excited.

"Don't try to drag me into your mess. You're sounding kind of desperate right now. Kelly don't know nothing!" Kelly said, looking up in the air, doing a ghetto-girl move.

"I think he's just trying to play for the camera right now. He'll say anything," Elaine added.

"Robert, the more you open your mouth, the dumber you sound. Just sign the papers. This marriage is over. You fucked my sister blindfolded, and you left the whole damn confession on her voicemail while I listened to you. According to you, you made love to her. Then you didn't have the decency to wear a condom. So what do you think, we're going to work things out and raise your baby slash my niece or nephew? Even worse, you fucked that nasty, crusty-ass looking Renee. And damn streetwalkers, Robert?! How desperate could you have been? You are stupid! Sign the fucking papers and get the fuck out of my sight and life forever!" I screamed with tears now in my eyes.

"What?!" he yelled, playing dumb. "But, Shawnee, this isn't fair," he pled.

Right at that very moment, the 70-inch television screen showed Robert picking up two prostitutes from a street corner.

"Oh yeah, let's talk about fair," I said, pointing to the television. "This would be you picking up two hookers off the street, which I believe is an actual crime. Isn't it, Robert? You're the lawyer, so you should know."

"And you know if he picked those prostitutes up, he does it all the time," Kelly said, adding her two cents.

"I'm sure the P.I. that I have following you probably has some more interesting footage from tonight to add to this video," I warned.

"That's invasion of my privacy. How could you?" Robert dared to ask.

"Oh, you're a fucking lawyer. Go get a clue!" Elaine yelled. "How could you seriously think the way you violated me wasn't an unwelcome invasion. You're a sick puppy. Not to mention all the diseases you have exposed both me and my sister to with your lifestyle."

"Robert, I'm warning you. You need to hurry up and get out of here before I lose it," I said, exhausted from the whole situation. "You know what? I'm going upstairs. There's your shit that I'm allowing you to have, in the boxes. There are the divorce papers for you to sign without contest, and get the hell out of my five-bedroom house that I'm so thankful I have never bore any children with you in. Do note that I said 'my house' since I have that included in the papers. And if I come back down and don't find signed papers, then we'll get to the ugly part."

Then I walked upstairs, leaving Kelly and Elaine with Robert.

Elaine snatched the ultrasound pictures out of Robert's hand. "Give me these pictures. You won't be keeping them."

Kelly was holding a pen in her hand for Robert. "Oh, please let this get ugly," she threatened.

He conceded, took the pen, and signed. He took the boxes out to his truck and finally left.

For the record, the ultrasound photos belonged to Charise. We had to play nice with her to get them. They came in real handy for the occasion.

So now, Robert's out of my life. I'll grieve and then figure out my next step in life. At least I have a fully paid house out of the deal and my freedom back.

24

Harmony

Well, it's moving day at last. I decided to temporarily put aside my differences and let my sisters come over to see me off. This would be our first gathering since the restaurant incident. Actually, it was Todd's suggestion. They'll finally get to meet my well-hidden man. Our girls' night out had long ago gone to hell. I guess it would require the resurrection of Momma for that to ever happen again.

I had a moving sale the week before. I prefer to buy all new furnishings for my new home. It makes for less packing, as well. I also donated a lot of stuff to the women's shelter.

"Boy, didn't Harmony keep you a secret," Kelly said to Todd.

Todd just flashed his dazzling smile.

"For a good reason," I answered.

"Well, I'm glad to finally meet the family. I was wondering if my lady was ashamed of me," Todd teased.

I playfully hit him.

"No, she was just trying to protect you from all of our drama. I guess she was afraid we'd run you off," Elaine answered.

"You got that right," I said, and we all laughed.

"She still won't tell us what state she's moving to. What state do you live in, Todd?" Charise asked.

"Please, don't answer that question. Trust that I have good cause," I said to Todd.

"Sorry, I have to stand behind my lady's decision not to disclose that information," Todd responded to Charise.

"That's wrong on so many levels." Kelly playfully pouted. "Fine, we won't let you know what's going on in our lives either."

"That's just fine with me," I half joked.

"Can we at least know what kind of work he does?" Elaine asked.

"Nope! Then you all would be on the internet trying to track him down to find me. I know you all too well," I answered.

"They wouldn't go to that length, would they?" Todd asked.

"Yes, we would," Elaine responded. "Oh, she knows us very well."

We all laughed and finished packing.

When I had a private moment with Shawnee, I asked, "So are you going to be alright, sis? I know this must be a rough time for you."

"To be quite honest, I don't know what I'm going to do. I have this big empty house and nothing but constant memories of the lie I had with Robert," Shawnee said with misty eyes. "I'm not going to cry. I promised myself I would not cry today."

"Did you make it to the therapist I referred you to? Surely she could help you right now as you sort out your next steps."

"What choice did you leave me?" she said with a strained smile. "I talked to her. She seems pleasant. But, the truth is I'm considering leaving D.C. myself. I haven't told anyone yet. I think I need a change from all the madness."

"Change is good. Would you try to transfer your job, or would you be making a clean break from everything?" I asked.

"Oh, I'm not that broken up to where commonsense went out the window," she laughed. "I've worked too hard to get my position, and I plan on keeping it. I'll be thirty-nine soon, and I'm not trying to start paying dues all over again to make it to the top.”

“Smart move,” I said. “You’re going to be fine, Shawnee.”

“I don’t know about that. Your sister will be back in D.C. sometime next week for good,” she chuckled. “And wait until she finds out that her husband has chosen to leave her pregnant for her younger sister.”

“Dare I ask? That doesn’t sound good at all.”

“Charise is on top of the world because Lewis professed his love and commitment to her. They’re supposed to be leaving D.C. to be together,” Shawnee told me.

“Never mind,” I said, throwing my hands up. “I don’t want to know anymore. I’m sorry I asked.”

“Tell me about it. We had to play nice with her to borrow her ultrasound photos that I used against Robert, and that play nice opened up Pandora’s Box,” Shawnee laughed. “It’s kind of hard to go back to us not speaking anymore after she helped me in need.”

“You sure got your work cut out for you. I don’t envy you at all,” I told her.

“Hell, I’m going to be following your lead real soon. You know I can’t take any extra drama right now,” she said. “And speaking of envy, Todd seems like a nice catch. He seems really crazy about you and well trained already,” she laughed.

“Believe it or not, I found him already trained. I didn’t have to do a thing,” I bragged.

“He has doctor written all over him, but I’ll keep that bit of info to myself,” Shawnee said.

I gasped by her accurate observation. Damn, was it that obvious?

“Please do keep that to yourself. You know your sisters would call every hospital in the United States to track him down.”

We laughed.

“You should be more concerned with Private Eye Kelly. Nothing gets past her always-digging self.”

"Tell me about it. I'm afraid for him to be over there talking to them now. There's no telling what Kelly has already assessed."

We laughed again.

"How'd you get a buyer for your house so fast?" Shawnee asked. "The way the market has been lately, most houses have been on the market for six months or more."

"Talk about luck," I responded. "It just so happened that someone had been eyeing my home for a while. As soon as they saw the sign, they were first at the door, and they qualified for my original asking price. I didn't have to lower my price at all."

"That *is* luck. I hope I get the same response if I put my house on the market," Shawnee said.

"Keep your head up, girl. Everything will be great for you. Just give it some time," I advised.

"Trust will be my greatest hurdle. My therapist will get rich off me just trying to help me with that one issue," Shawnee said with a hurting smile.

"Look on the bright side. You're free to have Eric now," I teased, probably at a bad time.

"Oh lord, please don't remind me of that fool," she said, disgusted. "He still hasn't given up. Hopefully, Sandy's return will put an end to his foolishness."

"You have got to be kidding? He still hasn't given up yet?" I asked in disbelief. "Wow, you're probably going to have to leave town." I shook my head, still not believing that Shawnee turned Eric out the way she did. "Hopefully, Sandy will have the baby in a couple of months, it'll be his, and they will live happily ever after, and leave you alone."

"I'd move before I wait on that day," Shawnee said in a serious tone before we both broke out in laughter.

After we finished getting everything all packed, we said our goodbyes, cried, and I was off to my new life, in a new city, with a new job and a new man. Good riddance to all my Wiggins sisters' drama. Goodbye, Washington, D.C.! Hello, Houston, Texas.

25

Charise

Kelly called to let me know Sandy will be in town by tomorrow. She asked me to steer clear because Sandy was coming with a vengeance. Apparently, Lewis called her with the information I provided him about the paternity of her baby. He took the liberty of confirming her suspicions of my baby's paternity. I'm glad everything is out in the open.

Lewis has been with me just about every night. He has been waiting on me hand and foot. He is so happy about the baby. When he goes out of town, it's because he's seeking a job in different states for us to move to. He said he doesn't want Sandy to mess with me or our baby. Wherever he gets a job at first is where we will move, and I'll be happy to get away.

When my sisters needed my ultrasound photos, they were so nice to me. They asked about the baby and even acted like they were happy Lewis chose to be with me. Since they returned the photos, they went back to their normal bitchy selves. They are back to treating me like shit. I was surprised Kelly even called to warn me about Sandy.

The way I see it, both Elaine and Shawnee can expect some mess with Sandy. I never did get the story of why they needed the ultrasound photos.

While we were at Harmony's house, I learned that Shawnee is getting a divorce. Probably so she can be with the guy Sandy is pregnant by.

I got the craziest phone call last night. I'm glad Lewis wasn't here. I don't need any stupid mess trying to come between me and my man. The idiot I met at Megaplex all those months ago called me asking if we could get together again. My stomach turned at the thought of being with him that one time. I'm embarrassed to know I fucked a two-minute man named Arnold. Who names their kid Arnold? I was all too happy to tell him that my man and I were having a baby and he needed to lose my number. He had the nerve to ask if the baby was his. I told him it takes more than two minutes to make a baby and then hung up on his dumb ass. Thankfully, he didn't call back.

Speaking of names, Lewis and I are trying to come up with some cute names for our son. We're having a boy. I bet he's going to have a big dick like his daddy. I wanted to name him after his daddy, but Lewis already has a son named after him. We have a couple more months to come up with something cute.

Lewis wants us to have a boy and a girl together. He said he wants his daughter to look just like me. I guess it'll depend on what kind of job he gets. If he can't afford to take care of all of us, then I'll have to go back to work for a while.

He also needs to get that divorce so we can get married. I guess I can count on my family not to be around for my wedding. I'm not even sure they'll come see me when the baby comes. They may hold a grudge against me, but they won't take it out on a baby.

Oh, I can't wait for my man to get to hold our son. I want him to cut the cord. Soon, real soon.

26

Elaine

"Heading out hooking again, or are you on the prowl for another one of my dicks you can fuck?" Sandy asked immediately upon my opening the door.

It didn't take her any time to come sniff me out. She showed up at my door just as I was getting ready for one of my paid dates. I don't know why I allowed my doorman to let her up. I guess I was worried about her telling him some stupid shit like she was saying at my door. Sandy has no shame and will embarrass the shit out of anyone.

"Welcome back," I lied.

Sandy is the last person I'd want coming back from somewhere.

Go back from whence your evil ass came, I thought to myself.

"Are you going to let me in?" she asked, while pushing her belly through my door.

"Sandy, I'm getting dressed to go out. Why didn't you call first? I would have told you this much," I said.

"You haven't answered my question, Elaine. Are you on your way out hooking, or are you going after one on my dicks again?" she persisted.

See, this is how bitches get killed, when they have too much info on your ass.

"Sandy, I don't think I need to dignify that question with an answer. And for the record, I apologize for my fling with Eric. Yes, I did know he was your past, but I had no clue he was still a present in your life," I tried to say firmly.

If Sandy smelled fear, she'd go in for the kill. Thankfully, she didn't catch a whiff of my fear.

She looked me up and down, twisted her tight lips, and then conceded, "I guess I can respect that. It wasn't cool, but I can understand your not knowing we were still kicking it."

Relieved she wasn't going to harp on the shit, I gave her a phony big hug and said, "You look great. Pregnancy agrees with you."

She smiled. "So tell me about this date. You're not still hooking, are you?"

Damn, she's still asking.

"Girl, please!" I lied. "I have my boutique now and am about to open a second one. I don't need that shit. My date is this guy who works at Georgetown University. He's taking me to dinner and the theatre." Another lie.

"You're going dressed like that?" Sandy asked in a degrading manner, while looking me up and down. "You know you look like a hooker right now, don't you?"

"Sandy, I told you that I was still getting dressed. I was just trying on different outfits." Also a lie.

"Well, you don't want to wear that," she volunteered.

"Thanks, big sis, but you know how I am when I'm trying to get dressed. You're going to have to go so I can go do my thing," I said, hoping she'd leave.

"You don't want me to see what you end up wearing? You're not fooling me, Elaine," she said.

"Okay, Sandy. Whatever you want to insist on, but you have got to go now," I said firmer.

"Damn, today is my first day back, and you don't even want to see your sister?"

"That's because one, you didn't bother to give me a call first, and two, you're not going anywhere. I'll see you any other day," I responded, now frustrated as hell.

"Okay, fine! I'm out. I can tell when I'm not welcomed someplace," she said with a raised eyebrow. "Make time for me tomorrow. We're having dinner," she demanded, "and you're paying."

"I can't do tomorrow. I'll be in New York shopping for a new boutique location," I gladly told her.

"Fine then! Call me soon. Otherwise, I'll be back," Sandy threatened.

Yeah, yeah, yeah. Now get the fuck out, I thought.

"Will do," I lied, while almost pushing her out my door.

"Hooker!" she yelled out as she was walking away.

You fat, evil witch, I thought to myself in rebuttal. *Damn, now I have to wait until she's good and gone before I can leave. I don't want her to see what I'm wearing nor my supply bag I carry.*

*****

The following morning, I stopped in my boutique to gather some papers for my trip and in walks Robert. I'm like, *What the hell?* After what we did to him, I'm afraid to be on the same planet with him. Maybe he was trying to pay me back with his own audio.

He walks over to me and said, "Can we go somewhere and talk in private?"

"No can do. I'm on my way out the door," I told him.

"Can I at least walk you to your car?" he pleaded.

"Can't do that either. I have a car service waiting for me. All this time, you could have just said what you came to say," I said.

I thought for sure he'd inquire about the baby that my flat, tight abs obviously was not carrying.

He peeped all around like he was worried about spies. Then he whispered, "Elaine, I need to see you again. I can't stop thinking about you. I don't care what I have to do or give. Just give me one more time."

Is he fucking kidding?! He's got to have a hidden microphone or camera somewhere.

"Robert, stop it before I tell my sister," I threatened.

"Please, Elaine, just one more time. You already know I'm as good as divorced. No one has to know."

I ain't gonna lie. My wheels were just a turning.

Damn, he fucked me wonderfully and pays okay, too. God help me if Shawnee or anyone else finds out about me fucking Robert again. Then again, this is what I do: play for pay.

"Robert, stop asking me. I can't do that with you. You shouldn't be here. You need to leave," I said as my weakness fought to take over me and my once firm voice began to crack.

"I'll give you another twenty, Elaine."

Did this man just offer me another twenty thousand dollars to get some pussy? Not the original thirty-five hundred? Whoa! That's a whole new desperate for Robert.

I have some regulars who pay hefty, but I didn't expect Robert to be on the same level. However, as much as I wanted to take the bait, I felt like it was a trap.

"I'll call you. I still have your number," I half lied.

I say half lied because after I think about how I can pull this off, I just may call him. If I can't come up with something, I'm going to have to leave it alone.

"Thank you! Thank you!" he said.

Robert kind of looked like he was on some kind of drugs, but drug addicts don't offer twenty thousand dollars for some pussy. Typically, my pussy does have that drug effect on folks.

"Robert, are you using drugs?" I couldn't resist asking.

"Drugs?" He looked puzzled. "Where would you get a notion like that from? I'm just a man who knows what he wants and is willing to do anything to get it. Your ugly-ass friend should have been that clue for you," he said.

I knew it! He only fucked with Renee to get to me, and when he got to me, he didn't need Renee any longer. Wow!

Damn, he stroked my ego big time. Got my pussy throbbing. Stroking my ego in itself makes my pussy wet.

"I'll call you, but I have to get going now," I said, this time more sincere.

"Please do call me. I'll give you anything you want. And I mean *anything.* I have plenty." He threw that in to sweeten the pot, but still not one mention of our so-called baby.

Maybe he found out it was a sham. I'd expect him to be pissed with me, not offering up twenty thousand for another shot.

"Bye, Robert," I said as I held the door open for him to leave.

I grabbed my things and hopped into the car service. When I got in the car, I called Kelly. I had to tell somebody. I also had to cover my ass just in case it was a trick.

"What's up, girl?" Kelly answered.

"Girl, you won't believe who just left my boutique propositioning me?" I asked.

"You're right. I'll never guess," she responded.

"Robert!" I answered.

"No!" she said. "You're kidding? How much did he offer?"

"First, he offered twenty thousand, and then he said whatever I want because he has plenty," I shared.

"Hell, for twenty thousand dollars, I'd say to hell with Shawnee and take the money. Just don't let her find out. Damn, what kind of pussy do you have, Elaine? Twenty thousand?" Kelly asked.

I couldn't believe my ears. Kelly must have been trying to trap me into telling her that I was considering doing it.

"You must be kidding?" I asked. "He's a damn lunatic."

"He's a lunatic offering twenty thousand dollars for sex that he's already had. Hell, I say go for it. It's not like you haven't fucked him. I'm sure you can find many things to do with twenty thousand or more if you ask. I won't tell if you do it," Kelly suggested.

"Kelly, why are you trying to pimp me out? I expected you of all people to be saying just the opposite," I said, confused.

She burst out into laughter. "Girl, let me stop fucking with you. You know good and well what I think without asking. Run, Elaine! Run as fast as you can. Run!"

"Well, is New York far enough? I'm on my way there now," I told her.

"I guess New York will have to do. Be safe," she said.

"I will," I told her before hanging up.

Damn her! She almost had me going there. Some way I have to get Robert to meet me in Philly. That way, if he tells anyone, no one will believe him.

So, after calling in a reservation in Philly, I called Robert to tell him what time to meet me this evening. I figure I can skip down from New York and be back in no time without anyone being the wiser. I gave Robert the wrong hotel info. When I'm ready, I'll call him back with the correct info. Call me paranoid, but I can't have him there before I get there, and I need him to have my money.

That night, when he arrived at the hotel, he paid, we played, and he was on his way happier than a kid who just bought the whole candy store. That was just about ten thousand dollars per hour, because he was out in two hours.

Now it's time for me to skip my happy pussy on back up to New York before I'm missed. Just as the first time, Robert did me well. Sure hope he doesn't keep sniffing around. It'll be harder to hide our indiscretions. Good thing I'm relocating. It'll be easier to do my dirt without prying eyes.

27
Sandy

"Eric, please tell me why you think my sister wants to be with you," I asked over the deliciously prepared dinner at Eric's loft. I went to confront his ass, but I wasn't passing up a good meal in my condition. "She has made it perfectly clear that she wants nothing to do with you. She's even talking about pressing charges against you. Do you really think she's worth going to jail for?"

He reached across the table, took my hand in his, and answered, "Sandy, I know this must be hard for you to accept. We didn't intend to fall in love with each other, but it just happened."

I raised an eyebrow. *Is this nut serious? He thinks Shawnee is in love with him? Maybe he's just saying this to push me away.*

"Shawnee does not love you, Eric. She doesn't even want to be on the same Doppler with you," I said, snatching my hand from his.

"I told you, I will still be there for the baby if it's mine. I'll always care for you, Sandy, but me and Shawnee belong together. And please don't be mad at her, because she didn't set out to fall in love either. It just happened," he said believingly. "I know Shawnee loves me, and I'm sure she doesn't want to hurt you with the truth."

The truth?! Could Shawnee be trying to deceive us into thinking

Eric's a bother to her, while she's telling him just the opposite.

"No, Eric, I don't want to believe that. When was the last time Shawnee was here? When was the last time you fucked her?" I demanded to know.

"That's information you don't need to know. I will do whatever I can to protect my girl. If she wanted you to have that information, she'd tell you herself. Being that she has not told you, tells me that she doesn't want you to know, and I'm going to respect that," Eric answered.

I was flabbergasted. *His girl? How could Shawnee be so damn deceitful? She had us all going with the stalking bullshit.*

"So what about us, Eric? Where does that leave you and me?" I asked in anger. "Not so long ago, I was your fucking girl."

"Sandy, let's not go there. There is no you and I anymore. Remember, you didn't want to stand by me when I told you I was going to start dancing so I could open up my restaurant one day. Now you're going to have to accept that I'm with your sister now. We will make sure the baby is taken care of, but there is no you and I, Sandy," he answered.

I was totally speechless. What could I say after that?

"Sandy, what we had back in the day was cool, but you know we never had a real relationship. If we did, you wouldn't have ended up marrying a knucklehead. What I share with Shawnee is real."

"You do know Shawnee is married to someone else, don't you?" I asked, because it seemed like he didn't know.

"That's just a small technicality. She'll be divorcing him soon, and then we can go on with our future," he responded.

"Eric, Shawnee is not going to leave her husband for you," I said in frustration. "What you had was a fling, and at the end of the day, Shawnee goes home to her husband. They have been together for seven or eight years. They are not getting a divorce."

190

"Then I guess you'll just have to wait and see, now won't you?" he asked callously. "I can't keep going back and forth with you on this. I already told you what it is, but if you don't want to accept it, then that's entirely on you. I let you come over for dinner because it just seemed like the right thing to do since you may be carrying my baby and all, but I'm not going to sit here and debate my relationship with Shawnee. Deal with it!"

I didn't know whether to spit in his face or cry. How could this be happening to me again?

"Well, if you were so in love with my sister, then how did I end up carrying your baby?" I asked with anger.

"First, it's *possibly* my baby, and second, that was in the early stages of our relationship when we didn't know it was going to be so serious. And thirdly, I didn't know she was your sister back then," he retorted.

"You know what? Fuck you, Eric. I don't need this shit from your delusional ass." I grabbed my coat to storm out.

"Yeah, I'll remember who the delusional one is the next time I'm making love to your sister," he yelled before I could make it out the door.

Damn, that was a low blow. I was standing back on the cold street of D.C., fumbling, trying to get my coat on and wipe away tears at the same time. Some concerned woman walked up to me and asked if I was alright and if she could do anything to help me. I did an *Exorcist* move on the poor woman.

"Get out my face and leave me the fuck alone!" I yelled as loud as I could.

I was so angry. I even foamed at the mouth. The woman took off running as the passersby giggled amongst themselves.

Why is this happening to me? The holidays are approaching, and I have neither Eric nor Lewis to share them with. I damn sure don't seem to have any family anymore. And I'm pregnant and fat. I couldn't buy a date if I wanted to. Something has to give. My men didn't leave me for other women. They left me for my own sisters.

I can't wait for Charise to get what she has coming to her. Not only am I going to beat her ass, but I'll be glad when Lewis dropkicks her silly ass to the curb when he gets bored with her. He hasn't stood by any of his other children, but she thinks she's going to have him. I'll drag out this divorce forever before I just hand him over to her.

I guess she was all too happy with herself by telling him about Eric. I couldn't believe my ears when Lewis called me to profess his love to Charise and the upcoming arrival of their son. He said maybe I could find happiness such as theirs with the father of my baby, Eric. He had already done his disappearing act. I don't know why he felt he needed to call me afterwards with that bullshit. Let him and Charise go fly off a roof together. I don't need his ass. The only reason I won't wish any ill thoughts on that baby is because I'd hate for it to come back on my baby.

When my anger started subsiding, I began to feel the cold whipping through my clothes. Then I was focused enough to make my way to Kelly's house. I guess I should have given her a heads up that I was coming, but what the hell.

"Kelly, I need some answers," I said when I walked through her door.

She looked just as annoyed as Elaine did when I popped in on her.

"Sandy, what a surprise," Kelly said half-ass. "What answers do you think I have?"

"I just left Eric's place, and he told me that he and Shawnee are still together and that she was getting a divorce so they could be together," I blabbed.

Kelly gasped in shock. "What?! What are you talking about?"

"Eric just told me everything," I said.

"Sandy, Eric is lying to you. Why, I don't know, but Shawnee has tried everything to get rid of Eric. That's how she ended up telling him about you being pregnant. She wanted him to leave her alone and figured that would push him to you instead of her," Kelly reasoned.

"So she's not getting a divorce?" I asked.

"Well…that's a whole different story," she answered uneasily.

"So how would Eric know Shawnee is getting a divorce if she didn't tell him?" I quizzed.

"That's what stalkers do!" Kelly replied. "They stalk you shamelessly and know all the coming and goings in your life. I bet he didn't tell you that he threatened Shawnee with the fact that he learned Robert's name and job location? That motherfucker is sick I tell you." Kelly motioned her hand to her head.

I made my way to Kelly's all-white expensively decorated living room and found a seat on the uncomfortable furniture. Her living room clearly sent you the message that you better not think about bringing any children in there or think about hanging around too long. You'd think for all she spent that comfort would have been included.

"You had to be there, Kelly. Eric was absolutely convincing. Even when I tried to tell him that Shawnee didn't want him, he went off on me, telling me I need to just accept they're going to be together," I said, shaking my head, not knowing what to believe at this point.

"Sandy, Shawnee is planning on leaving D.C. because of him," Kelly shared.

"What about her marriage?"

"That's done. Robert has a fetish for hookers. He was caught on tape," she told me.

Whoa! Not Robert! That's some heavy duty shit there, I thought, trying to process everything.

"How long has this been going on?"

"I'm not sure, but he's been neglectful and coming home all hours of the night for quite some time. I guess that's how she ended up seeking the comforts of Eric a.k.a. Mandingo. That is before she knew of your involvement."

"I had no idea things were so bad. I just thought Shawnee was being a selfish, greedy bitch. Of course, you know I know all about being neglected at home. It could run you into the arms of the first thing waiting," I said, pointing to my large belly.

"I can honestly say Shawnee has been having a very rough time, and the last thing she needs is for you to be going over there to give her some grief behind that psycho," Kelly said with her hands on her hips. "Speaking of psycho, you better pray he's not your baby's father. I would hate to think of his genes surviving another generation."

"Damn, that hurt, Kelly," I responded. "Funny, but that hurt. If he's as sick and delusional as he seems when it comes to Shawnee, he would make a scary baby's daddy. I would be scared to let him take the baby for a visit."

After some more small chit chat, I couldn't resist asking, "So what's Charise's story?"

"She's about as delusional as Eric. She has straight bumped her head," Kelly answered, leaving me intrigued.

"And?"

"Everything is Lewis this, Lewis that. And my man this, my man that," she responded with disgust in her voice, while rolling her eyes. "We have all made a point of staying far away."

Now I was really wondering, while getting angry on the low. "Is he living with her?"

"I couldn't tell you. Like I said, I keep my distance from her and the whole situation," Kelly answered, seeming sincere. "Look, Sandy, I know you have every right to know what's going on with your so-called husband and trifling-ass sister, but causing yourself and your unborn baby grief is not going to change a damn thing. It's easy for me to say let it go and move on, but I know that's unrealistic."

At a loss for words, I just reached over and tightly hugged my younger sister, who had taken a seat next to me.

"Thank you, sis. I needed to feel like I had at least one person in this world that I still matter to."

Kelly returned the hug and said, "You matter to many, Sandy. Also, you are three, almost four people's mother, and you are their lifeline. So, when you're down, they too are down. When you are up, they too are up." She paused and then continued. "Right now, focus on you and your babies, and everything will fall into place in its own time. Lewis will get his due, and Charise will walk in your very shoes. So, stop worrying."

"Babies? Those damn kids are almost grown. That's why I hate being so close to freedom and then have to be tied down again with a new baby. Hell, I wanted to go back and finish getting my degree."

"Well, better you having a baby than your daughter bringing home a baby, or even your boys bringing some pregnant teenage girl in your house," Kelly suggested.

"Girl, don't get me started. I try to put the fear in them."

We laughed, then talked for a bit more about Kelly's business and the kids before I headed out. I was getting hungry again.

28

Shawnee

What was I thinking? I was almost home free, and I had to fuck it all up in a moment of weakness. Now I have to worry about the ramifications all over again. Well, it wasn't like I had a little black book I could flip through. The worst part was telling him that I loved him. It came out in the heat of passion, and I couldn't take it back. So now, Eric thinks we are destined to be together.

My sign to run for the hills should have come when his stalking ass said, "Shawnee, I know you're going through this divorce and you need to be held right now. Please let me hold you, baby. You know I'm a sucker for your love. If you want to release all that pent-up tension and frustration, let me help you with that. Take this dick all the way up in you the way you like it. Scream, baby, as loud as you want until you have no more frustration left in you. Bite that pillow while I stroke you from the back. Have your way with me, girl. Beat on me if you must. Let me kiss all your cares away right now. I want to lick you from your tender earlobes down to your ticklish toes. Let me suck the hurt out of those big, beautiful nipples of yours. This is your meat here waiting for you to do as you please. Squeeze alllll that hot cum out on my dick. Don't deprive yourself any longer, Shawnee. Come get this. Come here and let me make your knees weak."

When he revealed his knowledge of my divorce that I didn't tell him about, he let me know he was digging and striking gold in his stalking efforts. However, all that other good shit he was saying made me lose my damn mind. All of my concerns of his stalking went right out the window. The alarms were blaring in full force, and I was suddenly deaf. The red flags were steadily waving, and I was just as blind as I was deaf. Now he's home wallowing in his bed, inhaling the scent of cum and perfume I left in it last night. He said as much on my voicemail when he called a few moments ago.

I guess no one could understand how much I needed that quick fix. Eric is like a drug. You know all the harmful side effects before you take the first hit, but still, you take it. And just when you thought you kicked that bad habit, here it comes in your weakest hour like your best friend in the world. Then, while you're caught up in the moment, it's the best thing that could have entered your life. But, when you come back down to the real world, you'd swear that was the last time. Never again, you say. That is, never again until that next weak hour.

Out of shame, I don't dare say how many times I went back for a hit of Eric's pipe after I announced to the world that he was stalking me. Any excuse was a logical enough excuse to going back for more. As strong as my sex drive is, I'm not sure why I don't go get some every day. It's hard to be big on morals when you're hooked on a drug.

Eric is my drug of choice, and I need another fix. Maybe once I leave D.C., I'll kick the habit.

PART THREE

Time Reveals All

29

Harmony

"Harmony Wiggins," I answered in my delightful new office.

"Baby, we have a problem," Todd whispered anxiously on the other end of the phone.

"Okay, you're scaring me. What's wrong?"

"I'm hiding out in my office, trying not to be seen," he said. "You will never guess who's sitting in the waiting room."

I thought and thought of who could possibly have Todd this rattled. I thought of his ex-wife, but that was done twenty or so years ago. For the life of me, I couldn't think of anyone.

So, I just asked, "Who? Are they waiting to see you?"

"No. She's here for the OB/GYN doctor."

"Who?!" I asked again.

"Your sister," he answered.

My sister? I thought. *Charise or Sandy would need the obstetrician, but Elaine, Shawnee, or Kelly could need the gynecologist. But why here in Houston?*

"Which sister is it, Todd?" I asked when I couldn't process the thought.

"Charise. Charise is here with some guy. Possibly the father of the baby, but I don't know for sure," he said, sounding desperate. "What am I supposed to do if she sees me?"

"Uh, uh…I…Uhm," were the only words that could make it from my mouth.

"You know once she sees me, she'll know you're here in Houston," he warned.

"I….I…I don't know," I finally said. "Why is Charise in Houston? She couldn't have possibly known that I'm here."

"Harmony, do you want me to stay out of sight or not?" Todd pled for an answer.

"Yeah. Yes! Oh my Lord! What is she doing here? There? This can't be happening. She has the worse drama. How could she end up at your medical center of all the places in the world?" I asked.

"I don't know, baby. This is wild. I'll just try to stay out of sight. Hopefully, she doesn't go in or come out when I'm coming out from a patient," he said. "I'll talk to one of the secretaries. Maybe I can get some information as to how she ended up here. She didn't know my last name or what kind of work I do, right?"

"Not unless you told any of them when we were moving," I answered, now trying to rearrange every paper on my already neat desk. My nerves were instantly shot. My delightful new office suddenly looked in disarray.

"Okay, then this must be one of those wild coincidences," he stated calmly.

"Too wild for my mind to imagine," I responded. "Okay, hun, let me know what you come up with. And please stay out of sight."

"Will do my best, sweetness," he said before hanging up.

The two hours that passed by before Todd called back seemed like an eternity. It was hard to focus on my own patients' issues. Mine were greater. Charise was in Houston! What issue could be worse than that?

"So what did you find out?" I asked when he called.

"I take it you didn't know your sister and her play husband moved to Houston two weeks ago? They live in the apartments not too far from the center. Supposedly, things were hectic back in D.C., and they wanted to make a fresh start with the baby in a new town far away from their stress," Todd said, while I was too speechless to say a word. "She's due the end of next month. That means she'll be coming more frequently. That also means the chances of her seeing me are greater."

I was at a total loss for words. How could this happen? Why Houston of all places? How do I turn my back on my baby sister of all people and still keep Todd's respect for me?

"Honey, are you still there?" he asked when he heard nothing but silence from my end.

"Yes, I'm still here. Just in shock. What am I supposed to do, Todd? You can't stay hidden forever. And she's here all alone with that whoremonger husband of my other sister," I stated on the brink of tears.

I really wanted to hurt Lewis for what he had done to my family. My emotions were mixed with every flavor. I needed someone to give me the answers to my life like I give to others.

"I don't have an answer right now, but how about a night out this evening and then we can put our heads together?" Todd tried to ease my anxieties. "You know I'm all for family, but I don't like any situation that is upsetting to you."

"It'll be my luck that we end up someplace they will be tonight, also," I pouted.

He laughed. "Well, we'll go somewhere too expensive for them to afford to show up. That should fix that."

I couldn't help but laugh. Todd is so wonderful and thoughtful. Most guys would have said, "Then we'll stay home." With him, I feel like I can get through anything.

30

Charise

Today was my first doctor's appointment in my new hometown, Houston. It was so romantic how Lewis came and whisked me away from all the troubles back home. He was gone for several weeks, and at one point, I thought he wasn't coming back, although he called regularly to check on me. However, he was here getting set up for me and the baby. He got us a nice two-bedroom apartment and made the other room a nursery for the baby. He furnished most of the big items and said he wants me to put the finishing touches on our home, just the way I'd like it to be.

I couldn't leave D.C. before Sandy found her way to my job to let everyone know that my baby was the baby of her husband and sibling to her own baby. I was so embarrassed, I couldn't return to work. Sandy has no shame, so she had no problem making a fool of herself, but she had to take me down with her. I guess I have the last laugh, because I have Lewis. I have my baby's father. I have a nice new home, and she has nothing. And since I'm no longer working, we have an incredible sex life around Lewis' work hours. Thanks, Sandy!

Lewis told me that Sandy said she will never grant him a divorce, and if he wants a divorce, he will pay dearly. She said after her baby is born, she will bleed his pockets for child support. I guess she forgot she's carrying another man's baby.

I love our new apartment complex. It's beautiful, nothing like D.C. However, the walls are paper thin. I met one of our neighbors yesterday, who informed me they can hear all of our sexual activities. When I told Lewis, he said he didn't care and that they could listen all they wanted to.

The neighbor I met is named Nicole. She is bi-racial and twenty-eight years old. I didn't meet her roommate Angelina, but I did see her through my window when she was going out the other day. She appeared Hispanic and was very attractive, as is Nicole. They both work and go to school, so they are not home much. I haven't met anyone else, just the polite "hello" in passing. I guess time will tell what Houston has to offer my new family.

31

Elaine

Things have been so hectic trying to get everything ready for my New York grand opening. Thanks to one of my "special dates," I lucked up on an excellent midtown location not far from Central Park, right in the heart of where the money is. My boutique has two floors and is very spacious. I've decided to use the second floor for VIP showings and my office.

I hired a publicist to help create a buzz. As a result, we have this grandiose grand-opening party with a celebrity-filled guest list of twelve hundred people. I have major fashion designers coming for my grand opening and plenty of cameras to capture it all. We're even rolling out a red carpet for the occasion.

The party is tomorrow night, and I have a million and one things to do to prepare. I have a bunch of shoe and accessory shipments coming in that I need for display during the party. I also brought Kelly in on the action. I figured she could use this event for her portfolio. I couldn't leave anything to chance, so I hired a more renowned planner to shadow Kelly on the down low. My reputation is on the line, and this is a highly publicized event. Nothing but high-quality footwear and accessories will pass through these doors.

I found a really nice place on Roosevelt Island to call home. It has a view of Queens and Manhattan that is to die for. At night, the Queens Bridge is lit up like a sparkling diamond necklace, and Manhattan looks like a scene from the movie *The Wiz* when they were dancing in Emerald City. I can even see into Brooklyn. I spend so much time on my balcony getting lost in my thoughts while absorbing the wondrous views. It makes me think I have arrived somewhere. I've definitely come far away from that silly kid in high school who opened her legs for any of those boys trying to experiment on real pussy. Now I have graduated to owning two high-end boutiques, real estate, a stock portfolio, and two vehicles. I'm a long damn way from the hood, and the part of D.C. I started in was just that—the hood. But, look at me now, all you hating-ass bitches. You called me a whore, but I'm the good whore that your man pays to fuck, and more than likely, it's your money he's using to pay me. Enough to pay for this wonderful view along with the one I have from my D.C. condo.

My Roosevelt Island condo is convenient to the city. It's also much better for parking my truck than in Manhattan. I could just hop over to the city by train or tram, and go from there. One of my "special men" got a corporate apartment in the city near my boutique for me. I use it to store Kelly for the time being while she's here working on this grand opening. When Kelly is not around, it's a meeting place for me and him. No one comes to my home on Roosevelt Island. You never play where you sleep.

My D.C. men who really miss me find their way to New York to see me. Right now, I don't have time to make for them when I do breeze through D.C. So, now, I have added a couple more very generous New York men to my roster.

I must say, I have some very generous tricks that helped make all of this possible, with the inclusion of Robert's forty thousand dollars a pop. Since our rendezvous in Philly, I've hooked up with him four more times, and I upped the price. That's because he started wanting more. I never had a clue his pockets were so deep, but now I know.

If Shawnee would have known before about his fat bank account, I bet she would've pulled out all the stops to hold onto her husband and not have him in the streets chasing pussy. Shawnee likes to consider herself a freak just because she likes to have sex. No, freaky is some of the shit I have to do to keep my freaky-ass tricks happy. Sometimes it feels good to the coochie, and other times it doesn't. Even more so, you can't be judgmental or make them feel like something is wrong with their desires or fantasies.

Hell, I didn't set out to take Robert from Shawnee. Their marriage was long broken before I was with him. Otherwise, he wouldn't have come sniffing out my pussy at any price. I'm just a businesswoman trying to get paid. Fuck all of that other bullshit. And if I can get my pussy serviced properly during the process, then that's an all-around win for me. Robert services the pussy properly, so how Shawnee could let his ass slip through her fingers will always be a mystery to me. Guess she just wasn't freaky enough for the man.

After the last time with Robert, I figured out why Shawnee couldn't keep him satisfied. He is into some freaky shit that he'd be ashamed for someone to know about. I guess he feels more comfortable with me as a prostitute, to know his secrets are just as safe as mine. It was one thing when he wanted me to piss all over him, but he took the cake when he asked me to shit on him. I couldn't get with that program. Instead, he inserted his fingers into my ass so he could smell and taste his fingers. Thankfully, I had nipped that whole kissing me in the mouth thing after the first occasion.

He also gets off on role playing. One moment, he's the bad boy who needs to be spanked, and another moment, I'm the bad girl who needs to be spanked with his "big" dick. I'm like, "If you say so!" He also likes to do the "stranger" role playing. We're supposed to be two strangers who just met and can't keep our hands off of one another. Robert would have me strap up and fuck him in the ass. It didn't stop him from enjoying my tits and my pussy. He just wants to be able to experience the same "wonderful sensation" that I enjoy when taking it in the ass. I'd be surprised to see what he comes up with next.

When we do meet, I still have him meeting me in Philly. I don't want him to know I'm in New York. He'd be a thorn in my side that I couldn't get rid of. As long as he keeps having forty thousand to give, I'm going to keep on taking it.

32

Shawnee

"Shawnee? Mr. Neely asked if you had a moment to come speak with him," my secretary popped her head into my office to ask.

"Tell him to give me two minutes, and I'll be right there," I responded, wanting to freshen up first.

"Come in, Shawnee, and have a seat," Mr. Neely said when I arrived at his office.

Mr. Neely is the company's CEO and founder. He rarely spends any time in the D.C. office. It's typically a big deal to get called into his office, but when I get the call, I always know he wants to see a little cleavage and a lot of legs. So, I give him his unspoken request. I think his old ass has a thing for young black women, or it could be just me who gets his 61-year-old ass all excited.

I hear the office gossip about me setting women back a hundred years, but who gives a shit what they think. That's why I'm Senior Vice President of Advertising, which makes me their boss. Bitches! They always want to hate on a sistah.

"What can I do for you, Brad?" I asked.

He insists that I call him by his first name when it's just he and I.

After he collected himself from drooling over the ample cleavage I showed and my healthy thigh that was exposed when I took a seat, he managed to say, "Shawnee, I understand you're looking to relocate to one of our other offices, yes?"

"That would be correct," I answered, shifting in my seat to allow my skirt to rise higher up my thigh.

I intentionally sat on the black leather sofa in his office, rather than the chair situated at his desk for visitors, to provide optimal viewing. His eyes took the bait, and he was reeled in.

"Well, I have one of two places for you to go."

I "accidentally" dropped the pen I brought into our private meeting, and he watched my bosom as I bent to pick it up. Just before entering his office, I undid a couple of buttons to allow a satisfactory view, without crossing the line and being accused of something unethical.

He choked and then stuttered, "You, you can either go to Houston with a twelve percent salary increase…"

I opened my legs just as I was about to cross them. Again, I shifted in my seat to make my skirt hike up, with the gripping leather providing assistance.

He got a handkerchief from his pocket, wiped his mouth and forehead, and then continued. "Or you can go to the New York office with a twenty percent salary increase, you know with the cost of living being higher and all."

I started fanning towards my bosom.

"I mean a forty percent salary increase," he said, watching my fanning.

I dropped my pen again, opened my legs as I uncrossed them, and reached down for the pen. Then, while seductively looking directly into his eyes, I said, "Just forty percent for New York and more responsibility, Brad?"

"Well, you're probably right. Do you think fifty-five percent is fair?"

"I think so," I answered in a girlish voice, trying to contain my excitement with a poker-face.

"You know I spend a lot more time in the New York and Houston office than I do here in D.C.," he informed me.

That was letting me know that he'd be seeing a lot more of me than the very few times he does in D.C., which would imply he'd want peepshows more often.

"But, as I sit here, I'm thinking sixty percent sounds more fair," I said, as I slowly opened my legs one last time to re-cross them while licking my lips.

After wiping his mouth again, he answered with a groan, "Oh, yeah...yeah, I think that's pretty. That's pretty right," he corrected himself, unable to take his eyes off of everything but my face. "So, New York it is! I'll get the papers drawn up for you right away."

"New York it is!" I said, still trying to remain straight-faced.

As I stood to leave, I decided to give him a bonus by dropping my pen again to let him get a glance of my backside as I bent to pick it up. I didn't bother to bend my knees; I did a stripper's bend. I wanted to leave a perfect view in his crusty old mind.

"I don't know why my hands don't want to hold on to this pen today. I apologize for being such a klutz," I lied.

"Oh, Shawnee, there's no need for any apologies. It happens to the best of us. Guess it's better you than me," he said.

I gave him my fake laugh with my hand on my boobs, for his eyes to follow.

"Well, thank you so much, Brad, and I look forward to seeing you in New York," I said, then leaned forward more than necessary across his desk to shake his hand.

He never took his eyes off of my cleavage that jiggled with his firm handshake.

"Oh, I look forward to seeing you, as well." He paused before continuing. "One more thing I forgot to mention, you'll have use of the corporate apartment for one year. After that, you're on your own. That is if you choose to use it."

"Well that's wonderful to know, Brad. I'll give it some thought and let you know what I decide on the apartment. Thank you again," I said and then left.

I couldn't get back to my office fast enough to rejoice. *Hmm,* I thought, *I'll get a sixty percent increase in salary in New York.*

The problem with that is Elaine is now between New York and D.C. The whole purpose of relocating was to get away from my family and bad D.C. memories, and start anew. If I chose Houston, I wouldn't have a sixty percent increase in salary, but then I wouldn't have any family to worry about.

I should have picked Houston. Maybe if I would have popped a tit out, I would have gotten sixty percent in Houston. Oh well, hopefully New York is big enough for both me and Elaine. I think I'll hold off telling her. She'll swear I'm following her.

33

Sandy

Lewis must be getting tired of playing house with Charise. He's been calling a lot to "so-call" check up on the baby. If he really gave a damn about the baby, he wouldn't have left me pregnant. My other kids are glad he's gone. They hate his ass. They probably hate me always having to raise hell about his sneaky ways and how he's always up to no good. I'm half tempted to call Charise just to let her know "her man" has been sniffing around lately. The last conversation ended with him telling me that he really wishes he could figure out how to be here when I give birth to "our child." Now it's our child, when before it was Eric's baby without a doubt in his mind.

Speaking of Eric, that bastard hasn't tried to call me once since I was last at his loft. I tried having lunch with Shawnee one afternoon so I could figure out what's really going on. She assured me that any relationship between the two of them is strictly in his mind. I wonder how he's going to feel once the baby is actually here. Maybe I should have let him feel this child constantly moving around. That may have changed his thinking.

If I didn't know any better, I'd swear I was in labor now, but I have another four weeks to go. Maybe it was something I ate.

Whew! Oh no! That's labor pain, and I haven't even packed my bags yet.

"Hello," Kelly answered, when I called thirty minutes later after what seemed to be my fifth contraction.

"Kelly, I think I'm in labor. I think the baby is coming early," I said through a contraction.

"Sandy, it's not time! How do you know? Maybe it's something else," she responded, excited and worried.

"I've had three kids before. Trust me, I know," I snapped.

"Did you call your doctor? Did you call Lew—" She stopped herself from saying his name. "Have you called Shawnee?"

"You're the only one I've called. My contractions are coming five minutes apart. I'm on my way to the hospital. I gotta go!" I said before hanging up.

I'm trying to stay calm. I don't know whether to take a cab or call an ambulance.

I think I can make it in a cab. Shit! I don't have anyone to hail a cab for me. I better call 911 for an ambulance. Damn teenagers! They ain't worth a damn or ever around when you need their asses.

After calling for an ambulance, that brought the fire and police department with them, I called Lewis to let him know I was on my way to go have the baby.

Damn, what was I thinking calling Lewis? I meant to call Eric instead. Now I can't call Eric to meet me at the hospital because Lewis said he was going to catch the first flight out and be at the hospital as quick as he could. That ought to ruffle Charise's feathers.

Seventeen hours later, Lewis finally made it to the hospital, and I was still waiting for this baby to get out of me.

I may as well have taken a damn cab. That would have saved some money.

"Sandy! Why is he here?" Kelly asked when Lewis came into the room.

"I'm here because my baby is about to be born," Lewis snapped.

Shawnee had to grab Kelly, who was about to attack Lewis.

"Stop it, Kelly! This bastard isn't worth our going to jail for," Shawnee said with pure disdain for Lewis in her eyes.

"Sandy, you need to tell him to leave. Either he goes or I go. I'm not going to be here with his punk ass," Kelly said, practically foaming at the mouth. "He probably just finished fucking Charise right before he came here. The nasty-ass motherfucker! What's he going to do, kiss your baby with Charise's pussy still on his lips?"

See, that shit hit a damn nerve. Kelly didn't even have to go there.

"Yeah, whatever! Then I guess you'll be leaving, because I ain't going anywhere!" Lewis said.

"Lewis, where is my baby sister? Where did you take and leave her?" Shawnee asked.

"She's back in Houston, but if she wanted you all to know that, she would have told you since she's been there almost a whole month," he arrogantly answered.

I was having mixed feelings on the whole subject. On one hand, I wanted my sisters here with me, but on the other hand, payback is a bitch. I loved the thought of Lewis leaving Charise home lonely, while he stays with me.

"Kelly, I want Lewis to stay," I said in between contractions.

The epidural they gave me didn't seem to be working any longer.

"You'd rather a lowlife, who left you high and dry while pregnant for your own baby sister, to stay here with you?!" Kelly yelled for the world to hear. "Fuck it then! I'm out!"

She grabbed her bag and was out the door, with Shawnee shaking her head in disgust behind her.

"Baby, I'm so sorry for leaving you the way I did. I'm going to find a way to fix it, if you give me a chance," Lewis said as humbly as he could.

At that moment, I didn't give a damn about forgiving his ass or trying to let him fix anything. What I was focused on was paying that bitch sister of mine back for trying to take him in the first place, and that was helping to ease the pain of my contractions.

"Oh, Lewis! Do you really mean it?" I pretended to care.

"I'll do whatever I have to do. But, you know we're going to have to get that paternity test done so we can remove all doubt. I feel in my gut that this is my baby," he said.

I just smiled before the next contraction hit, which caused me to call him every name but a child of God.

Two hours later, my daughter Sandraea was born. I would say our daughter, but I'm still not certain. The doctor said it'll be a couple of days before we get the results.

34

Charise

"You know, Charise, it's probably best that he doesn't come back. He hasn't been treating you too good anyway," Nicole said when she realized two weeks had gone by without Lewis returning.

"Lewis treats me very well. Where would you get something like that from?" I asked.

"I really don't want to stir up any trouble, especially with us having to all live next to each other," she responded.

"Well, you already put it out there, so don't hold back now," I said, waiting to hear what kind of dirt she thought she had on my man.

"Lewis hasn't always been faithful to you. It wasn't me, but I have personal knowledge of this," Nicole told me.

"As much sex as you hear us always having, I know you don't think he has the time or energy to be with anyone else?" I snapped.

"I shouldn't have said anything. You're right," she said.

Oh hell no! This heifer isn't going to put out some shit like that and back off it.

"No, Nicole, I want you to tell me what you know," I tried to ask as calmly as I could.

"If you don't think you can handle what I will tell you, then I don't think I should say," she replied.

"Just tell me, Nicole."

"Okay." She paused. "I'm not sure if you know that Angelina works at a strip club or not."

"No, I didn't know that," I answered.

"Well, before you moved here, Lewis was hanging at the club she works at, and he was doing his thing on a regular basis," she said.

"Okay, that was before I came here. Most guys go to strip clubs," I replied.

"It was there that he met Angelina, and she told him about the apartment you are living in."

Still confused, I said, "What's wrong with that?"

"Him and her were into things," she answered.

"Into things? What do you mean by that?"

"I mean into things. They hit it off, if you know what I mean. And when he got the apartment, they were together in the biblical sense every day."

"Huh?" was all I could say.

Now Nicole looked glad to get this secret off her chest.

"They were going at it regularly, right in the bed you now sleep in. Then he told her that he had to bring you here because you were having his baby and because you were catching a lot of mess where you were living."

She took a long pause while I was still speechless.

"Since you've been in Houston, he has still been dealing with her. Now he comes to our apartment to see her instead," she went on to say.

"That can't be. Lewis is home with me all the time when he's not at work," I answered, still unbelieving.

Nicole shook her head in disgust. "You're not trying to hear anything, are you? I've seen him in my apartment. I saw them together in my apartment, right in my living room, kitchen, wherever. I can tell you what his ass looks like. That's how many times I've seen it naked."

"Nicole, I can't hear this," I said, shaking my head as though that was going to make it go away.

"I know this is hard to hear, Charise, but it's the truth. I look at you and feel nothing but pity because I knew before you got here that you had gotten yourself caught up in a mess. Many of the neighbors know what's up with Lewis and Angelina, and they feel bad for you, too. The crazy thing is Lewis told Angelina that you don't even know where he works. He said he planned on getting a blood test once the baby was born because he knew you were hot in the ass before he touched you. He said if the baby is his, he's going to straighten up his act and do right by you. He said if he finds out the baby is not his, then you deserve what you get."

The tears were pouring down my face as Nicole continued.

"He told her that you are his ex-wife's sister, and you tried to seduce him since he first got with your sister. He said since he messed up by getting you pregnant, he had to try and do what was right for the baby." Nicole tried to console me through her words. "I know this is some heavy stuff to lay on you at this time, but I'd hate to see you let him back in and keep being played for the fool. You deserve so much better, and since I've personally had the opportunity to see what a dog he is, I can only imagine it wasn't you doing the seducing."

I couldn't even put together two cohesive words. What could I say? Do I believe her? Why was she telling me these things? I needed my sisters. I couldn't even talk to any of them anymore. What was I supposed to do?

"Charise, do you know where Lewis is?" Nicole asked.

"I think he's in D.C.," I answered through my crying. "He said there was a problem with one of his other children that he had to deal with."

"You haven't talked to him in over two weeks, right?"

"He said he would call me as soon as everything was squared away," I confessed.

"You don't see anything wrong with that? Why couldn't he at least call you every day?" Nicole asked with anger.

"He has gone a couple of weeks without calling before, but he always comes back when he straightens out his business."

Nicole shook her head and closed her eyes. "Charise, Lewis is not in D.C. He's here in Houston. Angelina told me that she saw him the other day in the store buying Pampers and baby formula. He told her his wife, not ex-wife, had their baby, so he was trying to do the right thing. He said it was a baby girl."

I was totally confused then. Sandy was due around the same time as me, and she was supposed to be having Eric's baby.

Why is Lewis trying to do the right thing for Eric's baby? What does he mean trying to do the right thing? Right thing by who?

"He also told Angelina that he won't be able to see her anymore because his wife will be coming to Houston as soon as they feel comfortable transporting the baby. So, I'm not exactly sure where that leaves you, Charise. Maybe he plans on having you on one side of town and his wife on the other side of town. That way, he can be a father to both babies, if need be."

"Nicole, I need you to go. I can't deal with this right now," I said, too stunned to cry any more.

"Charise, I know this is hard for you, but just know I'm here for you. I haven't known you that long, but I like you, and you don't deserve this. If need be, I'll be here to help you when the baby comes. You're in a big new town all alone. This isn't fair to you," Nicole said as she was leaving.

"Thank you. I appreciate it," I answered.

After Nicole left, I tried once again to reach Lewis on his cell phone, and again, the call went straight to voicemail as it has every day since he left me.

Not knowing what else to do, I called Kelly and shared everything. She confirmed that Lewis was present for the birth of Sandy's baby, and she confirmed the paternity test showed Lewis is the father. Additionally, she confirmed that Sandy was heading to Houston in a few weeks. She tried to talk me into returning to D.C., but I told her that I couldn't travel because I was too far into my pregnancy.

So now what do I do? Maybe once Lewis sees our son, he'll have a change of heart and know his place is here with me. I do know we're going to have to move away from Angelina, because we can't live next door to a homewrecker.

35

Kelly

"Charise finally got what she had coming to her," I said when I called Shawnee to share the call from Charise.

"I wouldn't have even listened to anything she had to say," Shawnee said. "She's been gone all this time and wouldn't even call to let us know she was alright."

"I know what you mean. I feel bad for her, though," I confessed. "She gave all of us her ass to kiss, and now she wants to call when her so-called man gave her *his* ass to kiss. Then she had the nerve to call the other girl a homewrecker, while not even realizing that she was the homewrecker."

"But wouldn't that be hilarious if that baby doesn't turn out to be his?" Shawnee laughed.

"I don't think Charise was seeing anyone else. She seems one hundred percent convinced that Lewis is the father, so she would know," I answered.

"Girl, pulease! Haven't you seen any of those talk shows where those girls are a trillion percent positive that the baby belongs to the guy, and then five tests later, they still don't know who the father is?" Shawnee asked, cracking up.

I had to laugh with her on that. "That is some fucked up shit there. I don't think that's the case with Charise, though. I think she set out to get pregnant by Lewis just so she could take him from Sandy."

"You have a point there," Shawnee agreed. "I think Charise had her sights set on Lewis when he first started making passes at her. I just can't for the life of me understand how Sandy could turn around and take his ass back."

"Girl, don't get me started. I hope she gets what she deserves just the same. Lewis must have some good dick to make them fool-ass women hang on in there," I said.

"The dick is a powerful thing," Shawnee said before getting quiet.

That last comment had me wondering what she meant by that. There was no point in asking, because she would never tell me if she was still fucking that stalker guy. Funny, she didn't even talk about him anymore.

"Changing gears, so when are you leaving?" I asked.

"Are you trying to push me out the door and have D.C. all to yourself so we can't see what you're up to?" she joked.

"No, I just can't wait for you to get to New York and run into Elaine. She's going to be livid when she finds out you're there with her."

"New York is big enough for me and Elaine. There are millions of people walking around. The chances of running into each other are slim to none," Shawnee answered.

"Well, take that corporate apartment your job offered, and you will increase those chances. It's located right up the street from the one I stayed at while in New York. And don't forget, her store is only a few blocks away," I reminded her.

"Yeah, after that slamming grand-opening party, it's going to be hard to resist going there for my shoes. I like the idea of buying my shoes where celebrities buy their shoes, also."

"But could you afford them?" I laughed. "She has a pair of boots in there for fifteen thousand dollars. Who pays that type of money for a pair of boots?"

"Well, I guess you must have missed the thirteen-thousand-dollar sandals," she answered. "What does a pair of thirteen-thousand-dollar sandals feel like on your feet? All the sandals I have end up hurting the hell out of my feet."

We laughed in agreement.

"For that amount of money, they better not hurt, and they better have a navigation system attached to always get me to my destination even when I don't know where the hell I'm going. She could sell one pair per day and close the store. She'd still be making out like a fat rat," I said. "But, you won't hear any complaints from Kelly, because Elaine got me two new clients from the party."

"Wow! That's wonderful! I guess if I ever need a loan, I know who to call on," Shawnee joked.

"Not you, Miss Sixty Percent Raise," I laughed. "How you ever pulled that one off is beyond me."

"I owe it all to Mrs. Wilhelmina Wiggins for supplying me with ample, perky breast genes and a perfectly proportioned ass to match," Shawnee replied as we broke out in a roaring laughter.

"While poor me is working hard for a living," I laughed.

I had been dying to ask, so I chose now to do so. "So have you heard any more from Robert?"

I never told about Elaine's call regarding Robert's proposition of her.

"Robert!? Hell no! What has he got to contact me for? I'm not Sandy, and I'm not interested in any reconciliation." She paused. "Ewww! What made you bring him up? I was enjoying our conversation."

"I was just wondering if he would go away that easily." Now I decided to test the waters. "I know Eric took forever to finally go away."

Shawnee got quiet. *I'm on to something.*

"He did go away finally, didn't he?" I just came out and asked.

After stuttering, she finally answered, "Yeah. Oh, that's done."

"I guess that's good," I said, still suspicious.

And just like every time I'm getting too close, Shawnee found some immediate reason to get off the phone.

"Oh, sis, I have to go. My secretary is trying to get my attention."

"Okay, then. Keep me posted with your move."

"Will do," she said, then hung up.

I know she's still fucking Eric. If I didn't know it before, I know it now. Damn, so he wasn't as delusional as both Sandy and I made him out to be. Wow! Shawnee, how low can you get?

36

Shawnee

I hate talking to Kelly. I don't know why she didn't just become a private eye. When she started sniffing about Eric, I knew it was time to go.

It's going to be hard leaving him behind, because he sure knows how to satisfy my every sexual desire and cooks his ass off to feed me. Kelly would die if she ever found out I spend almost every night with him. I don't love him or anything like it. For me, it's just something good to do. After Robert, I'm not trying to love any man, any time soon. I'm simply enjoying one of life's pleasures: the dick. A powerful one might I add. With all the cooking he does for me, I have gained ten pounds. Thankfully, it's proportioned. I'm sure I'll lose it once I leave.

I have yet to let him know that I'm getting ready to leave D.C. and him, as well. Based on my previous attempts to end things with him, I don't think he'd take it too well. So, it's best I just go and leave him in the dark.

The craziest thing happened last night while we were fucking, or making love according to him. I kept imagining I was fucking Mr. Brad Neely's 61-year-old, crusty white ass. Even worse, I was even more turned on sexually. While Eric was eating my pussy, I looked down and saw Mr. Neely, and although it scared the shit out of me, I had a magnanimous orgasm. Then when Eric was on top stroking me with his big dick, I opened my eyes briefly and saw Mr. Neely again. When I closed my eyes back, I had another explosive orgasm.

Eric was wondering what came over me because he said he never got such a reaction from me before, but he said he enjoyed it. Damn, I better stop flirting with that old man so much. Now I see his face popping up at the wrong times.

I think the whole exhibition thing must be a turn-on for me. The other day when in Mr. Neely's office going over some of the New York office's work, I unbuttoned my suit jacket, revealing my braless camisole. I didn't do it seductively. I just did it to be more comfortable since I was leaning forward and the buttons were constricting my movement. I didn't think much of it until Mr. Neely suddenly kept losing his train of thought. When I finally realized the reason, I decided to give him a peepshow on the down low. I did my famous pen dropping, knowing full well when I bent to pick it up, my breast would be fully exposed to Mr. Neely. I think my knowing it turned him on made my nipples harden through my camisole. All blood flow was now confined to my nipples, and they stood at attention, begging to be seen.

Mr. Neely obviously wanted another glimpse, because he dropped some papers, and I bent to collect them from the floor without his assistance. While he was trying to collect his thoughts, my mind was racing with thoughts of my hardened nipples being sucked by him. Talk about a wet pussy. Mine was so wet I was surprised it didn't leave a wet spot on the back of my skirt. I was actually longing for his fingers to make their way up my skirt to find my tropical oasis.

All of this was probably preplanned in my subconscious, because that morning when I got dressed, I already knew I'd be meeting with Mr. Neely. I think that's why I elected to wear a camisole top with no bra under my suit jacket. Although I always wear a thong, I enhanced the effect with a pair of crotch less pantyhose that I picked up from a lingerie store.

The first opportunity that presented itself, and without being too obvious, I allowed Mr. Neely a glimpse underneath my skirt. He couldn't hide his erection as he began choking. That didn't stop him from wanting to see more. He kept finding all kinds of excuses to get me to bend in various positions. I got a kick out of playing along. I even went as far as to sit in one of the chairs in his office that leans back and cross my legs like a man.

Mr. Neely turned on the television in his office and had me focus my attention on CNN. I knew what he was up to. In turn, he focused his eyes between my legs, taking in the full view I was affording him. I kept my eyes fixed on the television the entire time I watched him in my peripheral sight as he rubbed himself behind his desk. I slightly adjusted myself in the seat to cause my skirt to rise higher, enhancing his view. I had to do the pen-dropping thing once more. So, I uncrossed my legs, with a total view for Mr. Neely, and then let him see the boobs again.

When Mr. Neely had all he could stand, he abruptly ended our meeting, saying, "I'm sorry, Shawnee. I'm going to have to cut our meeting short. I have an important call to make. I just want you to know, you have some really spiffy outfits. Keep them up."

I thanked him, and then he said, "Perhaps we could meet over dinner when you arrive to New York."

"That would be wonderful," I told him, then buttoned my jacket up, fixed my skirt, and left his office.

Although I get turned on by the exhibition game, I don't know what I would do if Mr. Neely tried to take it any further.

37

Harmony

In Todd's and my plan to avoid a run-in with Charise, Todd found out all of Charise's appointments ahead of time and would stay away from the office. It broke my heart when Todd told me that he learned Lewis left Charise to return to Sandy in Houston of all places. It turned out Sandy's baby did belong to Lewis after all. I still haven't found out where in Houston they are living so I could avoid that part of town.

Earlier today, Todd was informed by Charise's doctor that Charise gave birth at 3:30 this morning. I want to go to the hospital so bad, but once I do that, I will have blown my cover and not only have Charise bearing all her woes to me, but Sandy, as well.

Sorry, Charise, I can't chance it.

Todd tried to talk me into going because he felt sorry for her, too, but I explained the feud between Sandy and Charise, coupled with Charise telling Kelly that I'm in Houston, which would result in Kelly telling Sandy. Then I'd be caught in the middle of a war with both sisters in the same town sharing the same baby's father. Todd eventually saw things from my view and said he'd get some people to check on her. That was a relief.

What a mess! What a mess!

He did let me know that Charise found a friend that has been very helpful and was present for the baby's birth. I guess that's a good thing, also. Especially the fact that Charise has made a friend. As far back as I can remember, Charise has never had any girlfriends. Kelly was as close to a girlfriend as it gets, but then, Kelly would often be so mean to Charise, who just seemed to find comfort in her own little zone. Now she has a new baby and a new friend.

This might be the makings of a new and improved Charise. Then again, with her having a baby by Lewis, nothing good could come of that.

38

Elaine

Boy, if I would have known business was going to be like this in New York, I would have come here long ago.

My VIP department is by appointment only, and there isn't an empty hour in a day. My VIP department is open until midnight, while the main store is closed off to the public by 7:00 p.m. The main store stays busy because everyone is trying to catch a glimpse of the VIP's that come through all day long.

I hired four buyers just to go around the world and find me the top of the line shoes and accessories. They are worth every penny spent. I hired Jason, who is the most flamboyant gay guy that New York had to offer, to manage my boutique along with myself. Of course, he came with a long list of credentials and recommendations from people in the industry. He doesn't let a person out of the door without spending over a thousand dollars. My average per sale transaction has been six thousand dollars. That's why I love him and would do anything to keep him, if need be.

My VIP's buy five to ten pairs of shoes with accessories at a time. My VIP department alone pays all of my bills. At this pace, I could open another location in no time.

And with all these higher prices, my dates are much more generous and less demanding of my time since they know I'm busy with the boutiques. Business has always been good at my Georgetown boutique, but it doesn't hold a candle to my New York location. I've even had some of my Georgetown customers take a trip to Manhattan to buy shoes. Both have high-quality shoes, but my Manhattan boutique has higher quality and a much higher demand. I did want to open a location on the west coast, but it seems like it's going to be difficult to juggle. Many of my New York clients fly in from the west coast to shop. Needless to say, they are putting the pressure on me to open up that west coast boutique. Who knows? Maybe I will in another year when I know things are stable on this end.

I'm not sure what poor Robert will do once I leave for the west coast. He's got it bad. It's flattering and all, but he's got it really bad. Due to inflation and high demand, I had to raise his price up to fifty thousand dollars. He replied, "Oh, Elaine, you're killing me," and then said, "Okay," all in the same breath. Now he has graduated to cross dressing. He likes to wear lingerie and wants me to fuck him in the ass. Oh, but he's still all man, and he services me just right when I'm done with him.

39

Shawnee

Damn, I've been gone for three days and already missing my fix from Eric. Oh well, New York presents a wealth of opportunities. There is plenty of eye candy right in the building I work in, and since I'm the fresh meat on the block, I have been getting plenty of attention. I haven't seen anything I want to get involved with and then have the possible headache of not being able to get rid of when I'm done with him. Anything inside the building or on the same block may be a little too close for comfort.

I decided to stay in the corporate apartment. I wasn't trying to have the headache of rushing to find a new home yet. Not only that, but I get to stay rent-free and save money, too. The apartment is not too far from Central Park and will allow me closer access just in case I start back jogging. The fitness center is right in the next building, which I'm happy about since I couldn't bring my home gym equipment with me from D.C. The furnishings are elegant, but nothing that I would have particularly went out to buy myself. Most of the furniture in D.C. I gave away because it was something Robert and I picked out together. Other stuff I just put in storage until I decide what I want to do with it, or where I will end up moving to.

Mr. Neely called to let me know he was in town, and asked to take me to dinner and show me around New York. I agreed. I figured in my boredom, I'd get a kick out of watching him drool. I had to search for just the right "play" outfit. Since it was cold outside, I had to find something to keep me warm while I gave my peepshow.

I decided on a brown wool skirt longer than a mini-skirt, but shorter than any professional skirt, along with thigh-high stockings, a garter belt, and no thong. On top, I went with a revealing cream-colored silk blouse with a half-cup lace bra that only covered a portion of my nipples. Of course, for the public eyes, I have a brown plaid wool blazer to match my skirt. I wore a brown full-length wool coat with a mink collar and sleeves to weather the frigid outdoor temperatures.

The doorman called to inform me that Mr. Neely was waiting in his limo for me. The limo was my first peepshow opportunity. He insisted on sitting across from me rather than next to me. That let me know he wanted to see something, along with the clue of turning on the light to see me as we talked. Once seated, I removed my coat and let my skirt hike up enough for him to see I had on thigh-highs. I then crossed my legs so part of my bare ass was exposed.

I guess the conversation was boring him so much that he turned on the television again. With my cue, I pretended to focus on the television. Then I made the too-warm move and removed my blazer, which gave him sight of my ample cleavage busting out of my too tight silk blouse. Strangely, it was actually kind of chilly in the car, which caused the hardening of my nipples. With my eyes still focused on the television and playing restless in my seat, I moved around until I felt Mr. Neely was getting a perfect view of the kitty kat.

When he wanted to see more of the boobs, he asked that I reach down into the mini-bar and get him a bottle of water. My reaching down caused my boobs to protrude from the half-cup bra and was almost fully exposed by the opening of my blouse. After handing him the water that was actually closer for him to reach, I sat back in my seat, giving him another bird's eye view of the kitty. However, when I sat back, my boobs didn't go back into the bra as they should have. Instead, they sat atop of the bra. So now, it seemed like I was wearing a silk see-thru blouse with no bra.

While Mr. Neely obviously was massaging himself underneath the coat on his lap, I kept pretending to watch the television while switching up his views of my ass and pussy.

Then out of nowhere, he just said, "Nice."

"I'm sorry. What was that?" I asked.

He caught himself and said he was talking about the television program. I just played along and said, "Oh," though there wasn't anything nice showing on the television. The program was reporting on a famine infested area in Africa.

By the time we arrived at the seafood restaurant somewhere near the water in Brooklyn that took an eternity to reach, I straightened up for the public eye. We went and had a very professional dinner, and no one would have ever had a clue of what came before.

After dinner, the time finally came when I had wondered what would happen if he took it further.

Back in the limo, again, I gave him a peepshow as he sat across from me. Three glasses of wine later, maybe four, I was getting bolder and hornier. I didn't waste any time.

Of course, we had to ride with the light on again. When I sat in the limo, I removed my coat and placed it on another seat. Then I removed my blazer again, seductively. I asked him for a bottle of water, and naturally, he had me get it myself. That meant the boobs came popping out the bra again. This time, I added a twist. As I bent down, I used a finger to undo my highest buttons on the blouse without him seeing. The buttons were already set low on the blouse. When I sat back up, I pretended not to know my blouse was open. Then I turned just so, where he could clearly see my naked tit. The air hitting my nipple caused the hardening of it. I then drew one of my legs under me where I sat, which opened up his view downtown. Still pretending to be focused on television, I opened my water, attempted to drink, and let some spill onto my bosom.

I only expected to wet my blouse so he could enjoy the wet imprint of my dark, exposed nipple. Instead, he grabbed some napkins and came over to help me dry myself off. Such the gentleman. At first, he ran the napkins across my blouse. Then, as he was wiping, his whole hand ended up inside of my blouse, wiping my bare breast that didn't get wet. Eventually, he gave up on the napkin and just fondled my breast like he was feeling one for the first time. Me? My eyes stayed focused on the television as he let out a moan and my pussy contracted.

My skirt was hiked up so high that he probably could hear my pussy screaming, "Don't forget about me!"

His stubby, old white fingers finally found their way to the cove, and when at the cove, he seemed to be digging for gold. I reclined myself back to allow him better positioning in the cove. Oh, what a service I did for myself then. By now, my two tits were completely exposed, and while he used his fingers to find hidden treasures, his mouth went to town on my tits. The shit was feeling too damn good, so I just let myself go with the flow.

Before I knew it, my skirt was hiked around my waist, and Mr. Neely had me bent over the seat with my legs straight and apart, while he crawled underneath me and licked my pussy as he continued to explore with his fingers.

He continuously chanted, "Beautiful. This is beautiful."

Then he came back around my backside and started licking my asshole. He used his thumb to keep playing with my clit while he licked with his thick tongue. My legs were so weak, they were shaking. Then he laid me back on the seat so he could return to attending to my breasts while playing with my clit just before his mouth went downtown to go in for the kill. He made all kinds of animal noises, which turned me on even more. I grabbed everything I could reach to try and muffle my screams.

I must have been real drunk or on some whole other kind of shit, because before I knew it, Mr. Neely's fat red dick was in my mouth, and I was sucking like a baby nursing for milk, while his fingers were deeply inserted into the depths of my cove. I didn't give a damn about the light being on in the limo and the possibility of being seen from anyone outside the vehicle. I was in a place of ecstasy.

Everything came to a grinding halt when the driver announced through a speaker that we had arrived at our destination. That destination was back at my apartment. We collected ourselves before the driver opened the limo door, and when the driver did open the door for me, he tried hard to contain a smile. He obviously knew or had seen what was going on, which is probably why he made the announcement.

So I'm all excited, thinking we're about to head up to my apartment and finish this thing, but instead, Mr. Neely wished me a pleasant evening and said he'd see me in the morning at the office.

I was thinking, *Ain't this a bitch!* I was actually looking forward to having his fat red dick in my pussy. I was half tempted to ask him to at least see me upstairs safely in my apartment. That way, maybe we could have stolen a couple of strokes. But, I just let it go and walked away feeling like a trick that had just gotten played.

Eric, Eric, Eric. Where's a good dick when you need one?

40

Sandy

As soon as baby and I received our six-week check-ups, we were on our way to Houston. Since Lewis had a good job there, we felt it was best for us to be in Houston. So, he found a big house for all the kids. He'd be a damn fool if he ever thought I'd let him bring Charise's baby to our house. People think that will push him to spend time with Charise, but I say he's not allowed anywhere near that bitch or her baby. I told him that I wanted him to get a paternity test as soon as possible, because if he found out that's not his baby, we wouldn't have to be worried about Charise sniffing around ever again. If it turned out to be his, then I guess we'll deal with it. I still can't stand his ass, but I'm not going to give her the satisfaction of handing him back over to her. Especially now since I know he's my daughter's father.

Charise should have gotten a clue when he hadn't bothered to go to her while she was having her baby. Instead, he used that time to collect his belongings from that apartment, leaving her and the baby's stuff behind.

He's been completely avoiding her and made me promise to stay away from her since he didn't do her right. Serves her ass right, if you ask me. I get a laugh out of every time I listen to the pathetic voice messages she leaves him on his phone, begging him to come back to her. I told him that he can't avoid her forever and that he needs to get the paternity issue out the way. He finally took my advice and went to see her about doing the test. Naturally, she went ballistic. I wish he would have allowed me to go with him. I owe her an ass-whipping anyhow.

41

Charise

I don't understand how all of this is happening. Lewis said once we got back the paternity results, he'd feel more comfortable with us being together. He said he brought Sandy to Houston because he needs to be there for his baby girl. He said he didn't give a damn about Sandy, only the baby. He promised he wouldn't let her come and bother me or the baby. He just needed his daughter closer to him.

At least he's trying to be a good father to his children, I thought.

I asked him about the stuff Nicole told me, and he said it was a lie. I wanted to believe him, but Nicole had too many facts that I didn't have prior to her telling me, such as him returning to D.C. for Sandy and not his other children.

The day we went for the paternity test, he acted so sexually deprived. He told me the last time we were together was the last time he had sex, which was the same day he left about Sandy's baby. He said he wasn't trying to have sex with Sandy because he didn't want to be with her in that way. Since it was still too soon for me to be vaginally sexually active, he asked for a blowjob and anal sex. He said he couldn't wait to make love to me again. Giving in, I gave him the blow job to hold him over until I was cleared by my doctor for sex.

When I didn't hear back from him again, I didn't know what to make of it. He didn't even bother to call me about the results. After several days of not hearing from him so we could go get the paternity results, I finally went to the testing center myself. I was told Lewis had already received the results days prior. After showing ID, they gave me a copy.

Somehow, something went wrong. The test results showed Lewis is not the father. There can't be anyone else. The only other person I was with unprotected was that two-minute jerk, Arnold.

He can't be the father because babies can't be made in two minutes.

*****

Weeks later, through phone company records, I tracked down Arnold. I asked him to do a paternity test and found that it only takes two minutes to make a baby. He's excited about having the baby. It's his first, and although he wishes the circumstances were different for us, he said he will always be here for our son. He even offered to move to Houston to be closer to the baby. He felt Houston was a better environment to raise a child than D.C. So, he came and got his own place, and now we share our son. He seems like a much better father than Lewis could ever be. I also learned he can go longer than the original two minutes we first shared, and with some coaching, he was able to do just about everything right.

I had to find a new place to live since things were turning ugly between Angelina and me. She acted as if she had a right to be angry with me, when it should have been me angry with her. Living next to each other was not a good thing. I also didn't want to stay in a place that Lewis used as his sex spot before I came. On top of that, I could have sworn I've seen Sandy doing drive-bys on me. I take it she knows that Lewis is not the father of my son, yet she still has it in for me. She needs to get a life.

I wasn't quite ready to play house with Arnold yet, so I found a place nearby his apartment. This way, we can share our parenting duties and occasionally hook up for sexual purposes. I don't know how this arrangement is going to work out if either of us starts dating someone else. I guess time will reveal all.

Harmony's Epilogue

Well, everything worked out in the end. Charise doesn't have to share a man with Sandy anymore. After Charise's OB/GYN realized how depressed she was, out of all the places in the world, she was referred to our office. Todd gave me the heads up that she was depressed behind how Lewis treated her and the baby. He said he didn't know she was referred to my practice in particular.

Although she wasn't referred to me personally, it took her no time to see the name "Harmony Wiggins" on the board. And there she was instantly back in my life. As I predicted, that opened the door for all of them to track me down.

I'm not too thrilled about her current arrangement with Arnold because it seems like a recipe for disaster, but I certainly am glad it's anyone except Lewis. I'm also glad she didn't move in with the guy. He seems pleasant enough and like an excellent father, but they didn't have the most optimal beginning of a relationship. Hopefully, Charise won't ever be so dumb to allow Lewis to worm his way back in.

Lewis supposedly rededicated himself to Sandy. How she could take him back after all he's done is beyond my comprehension. They started going to church together to help stay on track. Knowing Lewis the way I do, he's in church to see what other women he can find and will cheat on Sandy the first chance given to him. Sandy actually admitted that her only purpose for taking Lewis back was to get even with Charise. She said she didn't care anything about him. However, now with them going to church, she says she will see what happens and is willing to do what it takes to make her marriage work, even if that means forgiving all of his transgressions against her.

Kelly has been doing her thing with the event planning. She finally learned how to hire a competent staff, and she's traveling to New York and Los Angeles to plan events for some affluent people. Her home remains in D.C. because she's content having a place called home to return to. With her schedule being so demanding, she has no more time for dating. Perhaps if the right guy comes along, she'll find the time. Ironically, Eric found a way to contact Kelly since he could not locate Shawnee. Kelly, being the private eye in the family, was able to find out about their lengthy affair that had gone on long after Shawnee made claims that it was over. Kelly sent Eric on a wild-goose chase and told him that she believed Shawnee had relocated somewhere in Atlanta, but couldn't be certain since they were no longer speaking. She hadn't heard from him since. Maybe he went to Atlanta?

Of course, Shawnee denied any involvement with Eric to Kelly, but felt the need to confess her addiction to me. When Shawnee told me that she has been having sex with her old-ass boss as a substitute, I like to have died. When she told me that she actually enjoys it, it made me sick. She said it started off as just flirting, then it grew into the exhibition game, and ultimately, they went all the way. Supposedly, "it just happened." Yeah right! I think one way or another, Shawnee has been doing whatever necessary to make it to the top all her life. She claims this is the first time she went all the way with a boss. I guess for her, it's all worth it. She decided to go out with different guys she's met in New York and just wants to keep all her options open. I guess after all that she's been through with Robert, she's entitled. Particularly since she's open with her arrangement and not trying to deceive anyone into thinking they are exclusive.

Other than finding out that she is sharing New York with Shawnee, thankfully, Elaine is the one person who hasn't been calling me with something nasty or some drama. Elaine's shoe stores have been bringing her much success. They have been featured on one of those fashion television programs. I can't remember the name of the show. It was with some west coast celebrities talking about how they always fly to New York to get some of the hottest shoes and accessories. Then they gave the two stores a plug-in on the show, which only increased her business. She's even hired three more buyers for her stores and a full-time manager to work with Jason. Elaine is still considering that west coast location. I always wondered how she afforded to pull off these two high-end stores in the most expensive parts of town. Hell, we all received the same inheritance, but she seemed to have worked miracles with hers. She has always been a hard worker. Hats off to Elaine, I guess. Somehow she's doing it.

Angelo finally got up the nerve to share his lifestyle with the family. I had already softened the blow for him months prior. Although, he ruffled my feathers when he said he's considering getting a sex change operation and changing his name to Angela. I guess if there were ever a sequel to the story of our lives as sisters, Angela would have to be included. He said he's going to use his business degree to open up a high-end hair salon and day spa either in New York or Los Angeles in the next year. He feels if Elaine could pull it off, he could do it, as well. Elaine offered to let him run the west coast location if and when she opens it up. He said he'd consider it after investigating the feasibility of the operation he's trying to embark upon. I guess with Jason on staff, Elaine is finding the gay image is not a detriment to her business. Now she wants Angelo. Particularly since Angelo knows his shoes and knows of all the well-known fashion designers.

Todd proposed to me on Valentine's Day. Our wedding is scheduled for next Valentine's Day. We decided to marry at the same resort in Cancun where we began our relationship. I hope Charise and

Sandy duke it out before my wedding if they're going to do it. I'd hate for their first time of getting together to be at my wedding and then they decide to get into it. If it were left up to me, none of my family would be there, but since Todd wants both our families present, we can only hope for the best. Hopefully, Angelo stays Angelo long enough to walk me down the aisle. I don't think it would be cute to have Angela walking me.

After all these months, I finally gave Todd some, and it felt pretty damn good. I kind of wanted to wait until we got married, just out of tradition, but then I thought, *Who am I trying to fool?* I go to church every now and again, but I'm not so religious to where I learned to completely put away fornication. Thankfully, since he's going to be my husband soon anyway, he's open to the idea of providing me at least one offspring before my biological clock stops ticking. Todd's older sons are also excited about the possibility of having a little brother or sister. I will inherit a wonderful new family when we are married. I wish I could say the same for him.

The End!

(For Now…)

Thank you for reading *Between Sisters*. If you enjoyed this novel, be sure to lookout for:

Between More Sisters
Caught Up Between Sisters
The Evolution Between Sisters
Never Again Between Sisters
Revenge Between Sisters

Also, log onto our website at www.betweensisters-queen.com and take part in the *Between Sisters* discussion or see what The Queen is talking about on "Ask The Queen".

To find out what other books Queendom Dreams will be releasing and other authors with Queendom Dreams Publishing, please visit www.queendomdreams.com

About
The Queen

The Queen has been writing for many years, ranging in short stories, poetry, plays, professional, and other writings. She is a native of (Queensbridge) *Long Island City, New York* and currently resides in Nevada with her family. *Between Sisters* is her debut novel of the series. She is also the author of *Tapioca Pudding Next Door*. Her education includes Business and International Business. When she's not writing, she loves to travel to sunny climates with clear and turquoise waters or near the mountains for inspiration.